TIED TO A BOSS

A Novel

J. L. Rose

Good 2 Go Publishing

TIED TO A BOSS

Written by J. L Rose

Cover design: Davida Baldwin

Typist: Michelle Enos

Typesetter: Mychea

ISBN: 978-1-943686-62-9

Copyright ©2016 Good2Go Publishing

Published 2016 by Good2Go Publishing

7311 W. Glass Lane • Laveen, AZ 85339

www.good2gopublishing.com

https://twitter.com/good2gobooks

G2G@good2gopublishing.com

www.facebook.com/good2gopublishing

www.instagram.com/good2gopublishing

Acknowledgements

With immense gratitude first to my Heavenly Father for being the blessing that He is in my life. To the number one girl in my life, Mom (Ludie Rose), you will forever be my joy and happiness. I love you, woman! Pop's you know I ain't forget about you. I'm still trying to make you proud of me. I hope this is a start. Meka (Me-Me) Jones, my baby big sister. You know you'll forever be my boo. Larry and Kim, what it do, y'all! To my heart, even though I was a butt when we was together, Suzy, I love you girl! I swear the next time I'ma do things right. And last but most definitely not least to the whole Bryant family. I love y'all. Y'all who I didn't mention … keep waiting on it. Smile!

Hold up! I can't forget who made this whole thing possible. My new team Good2go Publishing and everyone who had a hand putting this book together. Ray, thanks man. I'm gone for real this time y'all.

Peace!

TIED TO A BOSS

Prologue

Staring out of the Burger King window, looking just past the parking lot, Alinna listened into the conversation between her girls. She looked at her Gucci watch for the sixth time in the past thirty minutes growing increasingly agitated while waiting on Big Worm's greasy fat ass. "Fuck this," Alinna said as she stood up out of her seat. Talking to her girls who were also at the table, she said, "We're out of here. Let's go." Heading for the side door, Alinna pushed the glass door open forcefully with Vanessa, Amber, and Harmony following closely behind.

In the parking lot heading towards her Lexus L.S 350c, Amber called out to her. Alinna looked back to her girls only to see Amber peering toward the entrance of the parking lot. "This fat motherfucker wanna finally show up?" Alinna said to herself. Staring at the Ford Expedition that was pulling inside the parking lot, she instantly recognized it as Big Worm's truck.

"So what we doing?" Vanessa asked her girl, carefully studying Alinna's face. She didn't bother to answer the question and started toward the Expedition. Big Worm's fat ass poured out of the truck. With some distance between them, she asked, "Who's all those other niggas Big Worm brought? I thought it was supposed to be just him?"

As they neared the Expedition, Vanessa said, "Just keep your eyes open," confirming that Harmony's suspicions were warranted. Cutting her eyes to Amber, Vanessa looked at the light-skinned girl who Alinna had brought to the team, realizing that the younger girl was focused on was happening.

"What's up se..." Big Worm started.

"What the fuck took you so long, you fat motherfucker?" Alinna asked, cutting off Big Worm. Big Worm's face went from a smile to having a unit on it. She continued, "And who the fuck are these clowns you brought with you?"

"Yo Worm, who does this bitch think she's talking..."

"What the fuck you said, nigga?" Vanessa spoke up, reaching for her waist as she stared at the man.

"Whoa, everybody just relax," Big Worm said, holding up both hands. "Let's just handle business."

"Where the fuck is my money?" Alinna asked, staring hard at Big Worm.

"Baby girl listen, I wanna holla at you ..."

Cutting him off, she said, "Motherfucker, if you stand there and say I've been waiting at this damn place for longer than I needed to before you to tell me some bullshit about not having my money, I promise you it's going to get real ugly for your greasy ass." She refused to hear any of his excuses.

The tone of her voice acted as a signal, as Big Worm looked around his eyes caught all three of Alinna's crazy ass girls pulling their burners. His eyes moved to Vanessa who was moving in, shifting a Desert Eagle to her right hand. "Alinna, come on shorty. This is me here," Big Worm pleaded. "I got your money, relax."

"Just show me my money, soft ass nigga," Alinna replied. Her eyes were locked on Big Worm staring hard into his eyes.

1

Fingers printed, pictures taken, and then escorted across the lobby to booking at the county jail, Dante found himself being led to a steel holding cell. "What's up with the phone?" Dante asked the female correctional officer who was unlocking the holding cell door. Running her eyes quickly over the freshly booked inmate from top to bottom, her eyes met his light hazel-green eyes that stared right back. His six-piece gold bottom grill gave off a sexy vibe that coupled nicely with the one he naturally gave off. The officer looked back over to the wall at the three phones, and seeing they were all being used, she turned back to him.

"Blackwell, give me a minute. I'm going to get you on a phone."

Nodding his head, Dante turned and entered the holding cell instantly catching the smell of piss and must. Hearing the cell door close behind him as he stood looking around the packed holding area, the odor grew stronger, and Dante was just about to find a wall to lean against when he heard, "Here you go, playboy."

Looking to his left, a dark-skinned, heavyset man with thick nappy dreads sat against the wall on the concrete slab that he was using as a bench. The man scooted over to make room for him to sit, and as he nodded to the heavyset man, Dante walked over and sat in the vacant spot. Ignoring the looks he received, Dante laid his back against the wall behind him catching himself. Remembering the stagnant smell in his nose, he snapped his head up. "Where do I know you from dude?" the homeboy beside him asked.

"Believe me dude, you don't know me," Dante replied, which only kept the fat man staring at him.

"Yeah I know you playboy," he reassured him nodding his head and keeping his scowling smile up. "I remember where I know you from. You were at Club Bass with this big big-as-a-house looking motherfucker. You got into it with that clown ass nigga, Prince. A woman told me you were one of them stickup boys." Not bothering to respond, Dante turned his attention forward only to hear the fat man continue. "They call me Big Worm. You ever get at that clown Prince for tryna shine up the club the other night?"

"Look Big Wave, or Worm, no disrespect, but I really don't know you and I'm not discussing my..."

2

Cutting him off, Big Worm said, "What would you say if I told you I could help you get at that bitch nigga Prince?" Big Worm proceeded. "But, I'ma need you to do a little something for me in return." Big Worm still maintained his scowl of a smile.

He began to speak again but this time was interrupted by Dante, "Understand something before you say anything else. If you plan on fucking with me, make sure we completely understand each other."

"Relax killa; everything is good on this end," Big Worm said smiling.

$ $ $

Three hours later, Dante walked out of the county jail after being bailed out on a first-degree misdemeanor that he received after being pulled over and caught with an ounce of weed. Dante walked to the sidewalk from the jail's front entrance and looked up the street when he heard a car horn blow behind him.

Turning his head behind him and looking down the street, Dante stood watching the metallic black and chrome Chevy Avalanche slowly drive to a stop in the middle of the street in front of him. "What's up, fam?" Dre called out from the driver side of the truck. Dante could hear the click sound from the vehicle doors unlocking as he walked up.

Opening the front passenger door, Dante climbed into the truck. "What's good bra, you good?" Dre asked his best friend who he considered to be more like his brother.

"Shit's good," Dante answered as Dre pulled off from the front of the jail. "Yo, this nigga Tony T told me to tell you to get at him once got out and that clown Vegas said he will check you out later on tonight. He said he's got some business that we're handling ourselves tonight."

"Nah, fuck all that. I got some business that we need to handle first."

"What's up fam?" Dre asked. Looking at Dante and smirking. Dante began telling Dre about Big Worm. He told him about Prince and how the fat man in the holding cell broke down some information about Prince to him. Just before that, the fat man made a call and bonded Dante out. "Fam, come on, that bitch nigga who was at the club popping that gangster shit with his boys?" Dre asked trying to confirm his recollection of this "Prince" dude. Dre continued, "The one who had all those thirsty bitches around him?" From the head nod that Dante gave him confirming his memory of Prince, Dre focused back on the road only to ask, "What time we hitten that fuck boy?"

"Homeboy gets home around ten so he's already at the crib, but were hitten him up when he leaves to go to his spot down south. The motherfucker Big Worm say's that every Friday morning around four, Prince leaves the crib with two duffel bags and two gunmen."

"So we're pulling an all-nighter?" Dre asked.

"Pretty much," Dante answered, and then added, "But first, I need something to fuckin eat."

$ $ $

"So what is this dude talking about, Alinna?" Vanessa asked her girl, looking from the road over to Alinna and into the passenger side of her new Lexus truck. "Does Kenny K have the re-up?"

"His ass is still with that little boy," Alinna replied. "He talked about coming to the spot and then his ass hung up in my face."

"It's time to leave that dude, Alinna – or rather kill his ass," Vanessa said, glancing over her.

"We can't do anything until we find a better connect," Alinna told her girl. "Once we find a new connect though I'm gonna make sure Kenny K's ass feels it for playing these stupid games with me."

Still heated and thinking about the bullshit with Kenny K, Vanessa pulled the Lexus in front of the Kenny K's trap house. Seeing his Benz E63 parked out front of the yard alongside a Chevy Impala, Alinna waited until Vanessa parked the Lexus and they both climbed out. Walking through the yard heading towards the front door, Alinna watched the front door open. She heard the comment Vanessa mumbled as Kenny K stood at the front door watching them approach.

"What took you so long?" Kenny K asked, staring directly at Alinna as her and her sidekick stopped in front of him.

"I was driving," Vanessa said, staring hatefully at Kenny K who completely ignored her and continued to stare at Alinna as if Vanessa wasn't even there. "We're here now, so you got the weed or what? I've got business I got too handle," Alinna told him making sure to get straight to the point. "You got my money?" Kenny K replied.

"You got the work?" Vanessa asked, speaking up once more.

Cutting his eyes over to her sidekick, Kenny K said, "You need to learn when to open your mouth or else I might just put something in it, bitch." He grabbed Vanessa's arm, and just as Vanessa flinched forward, two of Kenny K's boy's appeared behind him, staring out past Kenny K and straight at the girls.

"What's up? You got the work or not?" Alinna interrupted to offset the drama.

"I got three of them. Now, where's my money?" Kenny K asked, shifting his eye back toward Alinna.

"What happened to the five we've been buying?" Alinna questioned.

"I said I got three of them," Kenny K repeated, and then added, "You either want three or you and this tall he-she bitch you got here can get the fuck off my off my shit. Decide now."

Slowly shaking her head as she locked eyes with Kenny K, Alinna responded. "Where's the shit, Kenny?"

$ $ $

Seeing Prince and two more of his boy's enter the trap house, Dante and Dre calmly walked the two blocks up to the parked Ford Explorer. Walking through the front yard of the house that Prince had been using as a trap house, Dante kept up his pace as Dre jogged towards the front door of the trap house. He pulled out a pair of Glock .40's just as Dre slammed his size 13 foot into the front door sending it flying open against the wall so hard that the doorknob broke through the sheet rock embedding itself. Dante calmly stepped past Dre with his muscular 6'5" and 260-pound frame. They stepped inside the front door of the trap house and swung both of his glock's to the right.

Boom! Boom! Boom! Letting both hammers ring out and catching one of the two gunmen that entered the trap house with Prince, homeboy was just hopping up from the couch and swung his left arm towards the other dude who was leaning back against the sofa seat caught off guard. Just before one of the two rounds of the .40-cal blew through, his surprised expression and his face were wiped clean off.

Hearing the cannon-like explosion coming from his left and shifting his eyes to the direction of the sound, another explosion from Dre's .45 automatic sung out through the house. Dante looked back at the bodies on the couch and then turned and started after Dre who moved towards the frame of the bedroom door. "Let me in, braw," Dante urged. As big as he was, his wide body blocked the entire doorway. Dante stepped inside the bedroom after Dre calmly and smoothly slid to his right of the doorway inside the bedroom.

Seeing Prince's expression change as soon as he saw him, Dante flashed a sarcastic smile. "My nigga ... Prince, we meet again."

"Man, come on, let's not," Prince said fearing the worst from Dante.

"Looks like I am right on time," Dante interrupted, looking over to the two black leather bags that Prince had entered with. A grey gym bag also sat atop a king size bed that was free from sheets and blankets. Walking past Prince and completely ignoring the other two guys that were by him, recognizing one as the gunmen who came with Prince to the trap house, Dante stopped in front of the foldout table, tucking his left hand burner inside the front of his jeans, then reaching out and opening one of the bags, and then the other two. Smirking when he saw that the contents of the gym bag was money and the other two contained three bricks of coke, and finally the last contained multiple pounds of weed. "Prince, you must have known this were coming. Good looking out with these gifts," Dante said cheerfully.

"Just go ahead and ..." Prince started, but he was interrupted again by Dante.

"Braw go ahead and handle that for me," he said, gesturing to Dre. Meanwhile he slid his burner from inside his jeans and reached for the bag with the money inside. Just as Dre's .45 rang out inside the bedroom, ignoring the bodies that flew past where he was standing, they dropped to the floor. Prince laid there with the left side of his face missing.

$ $ $

Three minutes later, seated inside the passenger seat of the Ford Explorer as Dre drove away from the trap house, Dante ignored the sound of sirens heard somewhere in the distance. He sat listening to his phone ringing as he called the number Big Worm had given him to call once Prince had been taken care of.

"This Worm. Who dis?" Big Worm answered on the second ring.

"This me, where we meeting?"

A few quiet moments passed before Big Worm replied. "This Dante, right?"

"Where are we meeting?" Dante asked.

"Damn you already handled that, my nigga?"

"You plan on telling me where to meet you or have you changed your mind about the deal?" Dante said, becoming irritated with him.

"Nah, meet me at Royal Castle off 79th and 27th. I'll be there in 20 minutes." Dante hung up the phone.

"What we doing, fam?" Dre asked

"We're meeting him at Royal Castle," Dante said, pulling out a vanilla Black and Mild.

"We really doing the whole deal, or we doing us?" Dre asked.

Getting the tip of the Black lit, Dante took a pull from the cigar while he answered. "We will see how fat boy acts. It's up to him."

$ $ $

Still heated about the whole bullshit with Kenny K who was now seated at the table inside the bedroom apartment that she and her girls rented as their stash house, Alinna ignored the conversations with her girls as they broke down the two pounds of the weed they had just picked up from Kenny K, and bagging it up into ounces.

Getting up from the table and walking back up the hallway into the bathroom, she wanted to get away from her girls who were talking about Kenny K. Alinna was becoming more agitated with every word they said. She closed the door and looked into the mirror, holding onto the edge of the sink. "Shit, fuck, shit!" Shaking her head, Alinna took a deep breath and then released it when Vanessa stuck her head into the bathroom door.

"Are you okay, yo?" Vanessa asked. She was a big girl stepping into the bathroom at 6'2" 165 pounds, thick and curvy but with a muscular frame, joining Alinna inside the bathroom. Taking the joint that Vanessa had brought in with her, Alinna took a deep pull and held the smoke in her lungs. While releasing the smoke after holding it for as long as she could, she said, "I want to kill that motherfucker, Nessa, for real."

"Just say the word; I will happily get rid of his ass," Vanessa told Alinna, almost happily. Shaking her head on the account of how easy it was to get Vanessa on board, she looked back at her friend with a smile.

Alinna then quickly became serious and said, "We will deal with Kenny K first then plan on how we're gonna deal with this weed connect problem we got."

$ $ $

Reaching over and tapping Dante on the shoulder as he laid in the passenger seat with his eyes closed, Dre nodded toward the diner parking lot at an Expedition that was pulling in. "Ain't that homies ride?" Seeing the truck, Dante sat watching it closely as it pulled into an empty space in the lot. They watched Big Worm poor himself out after the truck was quickly put in park and the door opened. The other doors then opened revealing two more men who climbed out from the truck.

"Big Worm is a little nervous after all," Dante said with some laugher in his voice.

Opening the car door, climbing out of Dre's Avalanche, and walking around to meet sides with Dre at the front of the vehicle, Dante nodded to Big Worm and the five guys who were occupying the Expedition. "Looks like this nigga was planning a get together. Come on, let's go say hi."

Seeing Big Worm inside the Royal Castle, both Dante and Dre headed around to the front end of the diner to greet him. Dre opened the door allowing Dante to enter first and then followed behind him. Dante walked straight up on Big Worm at his table before any of them noticed. "You brought friends I see."

"Shit!" Big Worm said, startled by Dante.

Big Worm then looked at him and then to Dre, recognizing how big he was. "You didn't come alone either."

Ignoring the others who were with Big Worm as well as their stares, Dante pulled up a chair, and turned it backwards as he sat. "Here's the deal," Dante began. "I got three bricks and three pounds for you. I want $4,200 for the weed and $27,000 for the coke."

"Damn playboy, you asking for $31,000 from the boy? I thought we were cool?" Big Worm told Dante staring into his eyes and seeing how serious Dante was.

"Either yes or no. It's just that simple; you choose," Dante told Big Worm nodding his head and thinking about the work that was being offered.

Big Worm answered, "Alright, I call that. Now what about the other part of the deal?"

Holding Big Worms eyes, Dante asked after a moment of silence, "What's this problem you're talking about?"

Slowly smiling, Big Worm answered, "Her name is Alinna Rodriguez."

"Hold up," Dre had spoken for the first time since walking into the diner. "It's a woman?"

"Now don't get twisted," Big Worm responded. "This ain't no normal chick. She's straight evil and she's got a team of demon bitches just as evil as that hoe. She's got this bitch, Vanessa who's evil and crazier than all the rest of them!"

Watching Big Worm's facial expressions as he told them about her, Dante paid close attention to what was being told to him, but also the hatred fuming from Big Worm's massive body.

2

Two days after the hit on Prince and then getting off with the weed and coke, both he and Dre split the $31,200 from Big Worm as well as the $21,000 that was inside the gym bag that came from Prince's spot. Dante spent the first day after the second meeting with Big Worm at the Royal Castle searching for Alinna Rodriguez. After checking out the spot that Big Worm had told him about, Dante saw nothing and no one through that the first day.

He peeped the Lexus truck and the white Acura Legend on the second day of watching the spot. Parked inside the his marble brown and chrome 2013 Nissan Altima inside the same parking lot as the two other vehicles he was casing, Dante watched the four females as they walked past the car. He was instantly caught up starring at the 5'6", 125-pound Tammy Torres lookalike. He caught one of the other girls from the Acura calling the Tammy Torres lookalike by the name of Alinna. "So you're the evil bitch that got Fat Ass Worm all shook the hell up?" Dante said to himself, smirking as he sat watching Alinna and her crew through his midnight black tinted windows. All four of the girls entered into the apartment building.

Hopping out of the Altima, Dante closed the car door and headed toward the apartment entrance. Seeing the four of them heading up the stairwell, Dante broke into a sprint up the hallway to the end of the stairwell to keep sight of them. He then walked up the stairs and was about to step off onto the second level as Alinna and her girls were seen standing in front of apartment D17's door. Dante knew he was slick and they would not know or recognize him so he continue on and walked past as the girls entered into the apartment. Dante even caught some of the conversation the four of them are having. He met eyes with one of the girls as he was peering inside as he walked by; it was the girl who was the passenger inside the Acura as she closed the door.

Dante pulled out his phone to call Dre as he tried to sneak his way back out of the building as to remain obscured from following the girls.

"Yeah, who's dis?" Dre answered.

"What's up braw? Where you at?"

"At the spot, what's up?"

"I finally caught up with the chick fat boy has us on," Dante replied.

"Oh yeah? What does she look like?"

"You know that model Lil Wayne messes with, Tammy Torres?" asked Dante.

"Hmm ... nah nigga, oh hold up, the Spanish chick that's in all of those black dudes magazines?"

"Yeah she's in all those magazines modeling and shit. Anyways nigga, this Alinna chick looks just like her." Dante strolled out to his car.

"Okay so what's up, what we doin?" Dre asked Dante, confused by the excited tone in his voice over Alinna.

"Get at them clowns Tony T and Vegas. Tell those fools we're heading to Club Empire tonight and to get to my crib by ten, Dre," Dante instructed.

"Wait, what's up fam?"

"I'ma holla at you tonight," Dante told Dre. "But, keep this shit between us; we're handling this shit ourselves."

Dante hung up the phone with Dre and then looked over to the Lexus truck that Alinna had climbed out of with that tall, thick, muscular chick, while thinking for a moment. He cranked up the engine of the Altima, backed out, and went to find something to eat.

Back at the apartment and hearing her phone ring inside her purse, Alinna pulled her out iPhone from her Gucci bag. The screen read, 'MIGUEL RUIZ CALLING'. She stood up from her seat and passed the joint she was smoking on back to Amber. She walked into the kitchen answering the call from Sergeant Miguel. "Yeah Miguel, what's up?"

"You already know what's up, sexy mami. When you going to help me out with that little problem Alinna?" Miguel responded on the other end.

Alinna shook her head keeping all of her comments to herself. Instead, she said, "What you got for me Miguel? And you know I mean *business-wise.*"

Laughing and taking the hint again, Miguel became serious. "You ever heard of a guy named Giovanni?"

"Who hasn't?" she said, and added, "I've already tried getting connected with him since he's close but not too close up there in Atlanta. The problem with him is how can I get at him if he don't mess with anybody?"

"What's my name?" Miguel said in sarcastic tone

"Why, what aren't you telling me Miguel?"

"All I know is you are going to owe me big time for this, Alinna."

"Owe you? For what Miguel?"

"A few months back, I helped out one of Giovanni's boys that's high up in the ranks. There was a bust about to go down with the Miami P.D. and Atlanta P.D. Long story short, I called in my favor and got you a meeting with my guy and he's gonna introduce you to Giovanni."

"Miguel!" she said surprised. "Don't play with me about this shit ..."

"I'm not playing with you; you know I don't play when it comes to business," Miguel said.

"Okay so when's this meeting?" Alinna asks with her annoyance that Miguel had subsided into excitement just like that.

"He's supposed to call me when everything is ready, I will let you know."

"Please keep me on this guy, Miguel," Alinna pleaded.

"I got you sexy," his voice went from serious to something ulterior a little too quickly. "So, how about we meet up tonight?" Miguel slid in.

"I've got plans with my girls ..." Alinna told Miguel. Not willing to hear anything else, she quickly hung up the phone. She was still excited about the news. Running back in her mind what Miguel just told her, she headed out of the kitchen, back toward the girls to tell them the news, hoping Miguel wasn't bullshitting and could make it happen.

$ $ $

Leaving the stash house just before 10:00 and still feeling good after the news from Miguel, Alinna road in the car talking to Vanessa, heading to her townhouse. Of course, Vanessa continued asking questions about the possible meeting that Miguel was trying to set up for Alinna, distrusting the entire plan as usual. Once at her townhouse, Alinna climbed from out of the truck and Vanessa told her she would be back to pick her up around 11:30. Alinna stopped at the front door and unlocked it, peering back at Vanessa driving off and giving the horn a slight honk. As Vanessa drove off and Alinna had stepped in, she noticed something as she closed her door – a dark colored car parked a few doors down. She recognized the car as an Altima but she had never seen the car parked there before in her complex. It caught her attention mostly because it was still running and the parking lights were barely glaring. Alinna still peered at it while closing the door and watched as the car began to slowly pull away.

$ $ $

Circling the block riding back around to look upon the townhouse that Alinna just entered, Dante shook his head as he drove away. Dante wondered what type of girl Alinna truly was. Pulling out one of his Black and Mild's, Dante drove while deep in thought, and was just about to light his Black, when he heard police sirens erupt from behind him. He promptly shut the engine off.

"Ain't this some bullshit," Dante said aloud while putting out his Black, seeing a Chevy Malibu behind him as he pulled over. Watching the driver's door of the Malibu open up and the driver climb out, Dante sat and watched a Spanish woman get out of the car. She was around 5'1", 115 pounds, with a 34-26-40 frame, and wearing plain clothes. She approached the driver's side door, only to tap on the window.

"What's the problem, officer?" Dante asked after letting down his window.

"It's *Sergeant*," she corrected him with a slight Spanish accent. "Can you please step out of the vehicle Mr. Blackwell?" Dante was caught off guard after hearing her refer to him by name.

"Can I ask what this is about, Sergeant?" he asked.

"I am going to ask you one more time Mr. Blackwell to please step out of the vehicle," she ordered while staring directly into his eyes. She reached back to settle her right hand onto her sidearm.

He cursed under his breath as he thought of his heater he also had with him. "Excuse me ..." Dante began to say to buy himself some time.

Cutting him off, the sergeant spoke again, "Dante, get out of the fucking car. You're not in any trouble, *yet!*"

Now Dante clearly had a look of question on his face. He truly began to wonder who this chick was. He climbed out of the car slowly and kept his eyes on her. The tone lightened when she looked him up and down; he had to smirk.

"Damn, you're finer than I thought you would be," she said, meeting her eyes with his. "Do you want to know who I am?" she asked.

"That would be nice."

"I am the one person who is going to keep you from seeing the inside of a jail cell or any other lockup again, but there is something you have to give me in return for helping you. You would be free to continue robbing others, such as you and your friend Andre did two nights ago; when you both kicked in the front door of Steve Washington."

"Steve who?" Dante questioned hearing every word she was saying.

"I am sorry you may have known him by Prince, am I right?" the sergeant asked while taking a step forward, staring into his eyes still, and reaching between his legs to grip his package nice and tight.

"I count on you, whenever I want it, every time I want it. That's in exchange for me making sure you are clear to run the streets with a pass to do whatever you want. Exactly as you did two nights ago. Do we have a deal?"

3

Making it out to Club Empire just before midnight, Amber and Harmony followed behind Vanessa in her Lexus as they pulled inside the parking lot. Alinna expected the club to be packed, but was stunned at how many people were actually there. She saw that the waiting line was nearly stretched around the side of the club building. Once Vanessa parked the truck, Alinna climbed out of the Lexus and onto her Gucci stiletto heels that went well with her skin-tight Gucci jeans and top. Walking around to the back end of the truck just as both Amber and Harmony came walking up from out of the Dodge Magnum, Alinna looked over to her left and saw a group of three guys walking past and staring in their direction. "I know damn well we are not about to be waiting out in this big ass crowd to get into no club," Vanessa said with her face balled up.

Alinna smiled as she bumped into her girl playfully and said, "Vanessa, just lighten up a little tonight, okay? We're here to relax and chill out."

"Whatever, Alinna," she replied knowing that she always carried that attitude.

"Look at this bullshit!" Vanessa said to herself, looking around at all the people.

Alinna heard her but ignored the comment. She was trying to think while looking at the herd of people in line when she heard someone call her name. "Alinna!" was heard over the crowd of random chatter. She looked to her right just as Amber got her attention, "Hey, the doorman. He's yelling for you." Seeing the doorman waving toward the front of the crowd motioning for them to come forward to the front of the line, Alinna motioned for the girls to follow her, holding onto one another as they moved through the crowd toward the front.

Noticing the light brown-skinned guy in the black metallic jeans with a brown and cream shirt underneath a polo sweater, Alinna caught the entire exchange in words and the head nods between the guy and the doorman just as she and her girls walked up. "You good shorty. Y'all can go ahead and go in," Alinna heard the doorman yell to them over the club music blaring from inside. She was listening to the doorman but looking at the nicely dress light skin guy, he looked back at her and gave her a wink then entered into the club.

"Alinna, who you know over here? How did you do that?" Amber asked as they walked in the doors.

"I didn't," answered Alinna. "I think we have a friend."

"A what?" questioned Vanessa, yelling over the music. Waiving off Vanessa's question already knowing how Vanessa was, Alinna lead them all towards the bar. Meanwhile she kept her eyes open, searching for that guy from the front door.

$ $ $

"They're here," Dante said walking up beside Dre at the bar across the club.

"Where at?" Dre asked as he passed a bottle of Corona to Dante. Taking the bottle, he leaned back against the edge of the bar and nodded over across the club over by the bar by the front door.

"The four females at the front bar, the one with them tight ass jeans on and the long curly haired woman is Alinna."

"Baby girl got ass back there!" Dre said causing Dante to cut his eyes over to him. He noticed the tall, thick, amazon-brown skin female that was standing with the

Alinna chick. Dre began, "Shorty standing next to Alinna, the tall thick one. She with ya girl too, fam?"

"Yeah, I think that one is Vanessa," Dante said just as Alinna looked their way and then looked past them only to snap her head back in his direction, staring at him.

"Ooh she's watching you now, fam," Dre said, her stare was direct and continuous right at Dante.

$ $ $

She found that guy from the front door staring at him across the club as he leaned against the bar staring directly back at her while talking to a tall muscular guy. Alinna looked to her right at Vanessa when she heard her ask, "What the hell you staring at?"

"Nothing," she replied, turning back to look over at the guy only to find him and the big guy were gone.

Alinna looked around for him but she quickly realized what she was doing and turned her attention back to Vanessa. She noticed both Amber and Harmony a little ways away but there was a crowd of guys blocking their way back over to her and Vanessa. "Come on," Alinna told Vanessa, seeing Amber snatch her arm away from one of the guys.

Walking up to her girls and the guys giving them problems, Alinna stopped in front of the guy who was touching Amber, "Is there a reason why you grabbing all up on my girl?"

"Damn," one of the guys had said smiling, as he looked Alinna up and down. "You're even badder then her. What's your name sexy?"

"Trouble," Vanessa, answered up as she slid up beside Alinna. "My advice is that you clowns keep it moving."

"Who the fuck is you? You he-she bit-" Before the homie could finish insulting Vanessa, she smashed her fist straight into the guy's mouth, sending him back staggering.

"BITCH. WHAT THE ..." a glass exploded as Alinna snatched up a beer bottle and swung it, smashing it across the across the head of the guy who called Vanessa a bitch. Alinna dropped the bottle and swung her fist punching the guy with the bottle straight in his nose.

Feeling hands grab her arm as another one of the four guy's jumped into the action, Alinna began to swing. A huge fist went past her and connected with the guy holding onto her arm, throwing him back into his friends. Recognizing the muscular guy, but locking in again on the dude from the front door, Alinna kept her eyes on him as he calmly walked out in front of her, her girls, and the his big muscular friend.

"Is there a problem here fellas?" Dante asked looking on from one guy to the next.

"Naw, Dante man, these bitches just ..."

"BITCH, NIGGA! CALL US BITCHES ONE MORE TIME!" Vanessa roared. "I promise ya ass won't leave this club alive!" Walking up on the guys again as if round two was about to commence.

"Apologize," Dante told the guy. Hearing the clown and his boy's apologize, Alinna stood watching as the four guys with him quickly rushed off after they apologized as if someone had started shooting. She turned her attention back to a guy who got them in and looked out for them. He walked away with the large man. Before Alinna could speak, she reached out and grabbed the light-skinned guy by the arm, stopping him. "You just gonna leave now?" Alinna asked.

Turning his head meeting eyes with Alinna golden brown eyes, he replied, "What reason do I have to stay?"

"So you're just gonna jump in for me and my girls and just leave just like that?" Alinna stared into his eyes examining him up close, noticing the six-pack gold grill that for some reason was sexy. "Who the hell are you anyway?"

"You will find out," Dante told her. "Aye, you may want to pay attention to what's going on around you."

Watching both guys walk away noticing the way people looked at them and moved as to get out their way as they walked past, Vanessa stepped up to be side by side with Alinna. "Who are they supposed to be?" Vanessa questioned.

"I'm still wondering the same thing," Alinna answered, she was thinking hard on the well-dressed stranger, and the so-called advice he had just given her.

$ $ $

"Yooooo, what's up fam? What was that shit about just now?" Vegas asked as both he and Tony T met up in the club with Dante and Dre, halfway back to the far side of the bar.

"It ain't nothing," Dante assured him as he leaned back over against the bar.

"Fam, what's up? What you plotting?" Dre asked Dante while watching him staring at the other side of the club back to the direction of Alinna and her girls. She was watching him watch her as well.

After a pause and awaiting a response, Dante said, "Change of plans."

"Fuck is you talking about?" Tony T asked, looking back and forth to Dre and Dante, completely unaware of any plans.

"Dre will explain," Dante told Tony T, and then he dapped up with Dre, Tony T, and Vegas. "I'ma hit you up later. I got something to handle right quick." Dre walked off leaving his boys watching him as he made his way back over to the other side of the club. Walking up on Alinna as she and her girls were talking interrupting them all, he said, "Let's go."

"She's not going no ..."

"Shut up." Dante wouldn't hearing what Vanessa had to argue. "I don't want you to say any other shit," he finished. Looking at her girl surprised, Vanessa was quiet and simply staring at the guy.

Alinna looked back at him and asked, "Who are you?"

"This ain't questions and answers," Dante told her. "Let's go Alinna, we gotta talk."

$ $ $

"Who the hell are you?" Alinna asked as she and Dante left the club together. Walking through the parking lot, she asked, "How do you know my name?" Dante ignored Alinna as he walked them to his Altima hitting the remote locks.

Dante walked around to his driver's side door when Alinna said from behind him, "You were at my house earlier! I saw your car. WHO THE FUCK ARE YOU?"

"Get in the car Alinna." He stood next to his opened door.

"I am not going nowhere with you!"

"Get the fuck in the car girl!" Dante was getting irritated with her.

"Nigga who are you yelling at?" Alinna became stern, looking at Dante as if he was crazy.

Walking over to Alinna stopping directly in front of her, bending to speak to her face to face, Dante said in a lowered voice, "Woman, I don't like repeating myself. If you don't get in the car, I will put your ass in the car. Decide now." Staring into his eyes for several moments, Alinna sucked her teeth pushing past Dante as she walked over, and got into the Altima. Dante shook his head, walked to the driver's side, and got inside the car.

Once Dante cranked up the engine and started to pull out of the club parking lot, Alinna demanded, "You really need to tell me who the hell you are and what is going on."

Cutting his eyes to Alinna as he was driving and focusing back on the road, he said, "My name is Dante, but, you got a problem you don't even know about."

"What problem? What the fuck are you talking about? What is this problem I got?"

"*Me,*" Dante spoke clearly.

Staring at Dante for a moment, Alinna asked, "What's going on? How do I have a problem with you? I don't even know you."

"You don't know me, but you know the dude who hired me to get at you."

"Hired you? Hired you to do what? To do what? What's their name?" Alinna was not liking this game.

"Big Worm," he said, looking over and seeing her reaction to the name. "Whatever problem you two got going on with one another, he wants you out the picture; *permanently.*"

"You some sort of hitman or something?" she asked looking over to Dante.

"I got a few bodies but I ain't no hitman," Dante told her. "I get mine the stick 'em up way."

"So you a jack boy then?" Alinna asked really looking him over now. "As a matter of fact, I have heard of you now that I know what you're into. You got them gangsta's out here all shook up."

Ignoring the comment, Dante said, "Whatever you and this fat clown Big Worm got going on, he wants me to take care of you."

"So that's what this is all about? You gonna take care of me for another nigga?" she asked, wishing she had her .380 with her instead of in her truck.

"Believe me, if I was going to kill you, you would have been dead back at that apartment on sixty second street where you and girls supposedly work," Dante said, looking between her and the road.

"How long have you been watching me?"

"Long enough."

He pulled his car over to the side of the road just to stop in front of a KFC. "What are you doing?" Alinna asked as she watched Dante put the car in park and get out. Looking back through the window following him with her eyes, she saw Vanessa.

The Lexus truck pulled up behind them. Dante walked up to the driver's door and swung it open. Alinna climbed out after seeing Dante and Vanessa get in each other's face. Rushing over to both her girl and Dante, Alinna got in between the two with her back to Vanessa. "Dante, what the hell is wrong with you?"

"I don't like being followed," Dante replied while keeping his eye locked onto Vanessa's.

"Nigga, I was not following you. I am following my girl. We don't even know you dude," Vanessa told Dante, reading from his demeanor how heated he was.

"Look," Alinna said loud enough to get both Dante's and Vanessa's attention. "We are in the middle of the street causing a damn scene. Let's just go in this damn KFC and we can just talk about this shit."

Shaking his head, Dante turned and headed back over to his car. He hopped inside the Altima and slammed his door, pulling off only to swing the Altima into the KFC parking lot.

4

Seated at a window table inside the KFC overlooking the parking lot, both Alinna and Vanessa sat discussing the news Dante told her about Big Worm putting a hit out on her.

"So why is he telling you all this instead of doing what he's being paid to do?" Vanessa asked her girl.

"Probably because I'm not getting paid for it," Dante said as he walked up to their table, setting a tray with a box of chicken down on the table with a drink in his hand.

"So if you're not getting paid for it then why you doing Big Worm's dirty work?" Vanessa asked, watching Dante sitting down inside the chair across from her and Alinna.

Pulling out a piece of chicken breast from the box, Dante bit into the chicken, and then said, "It was a favor he did for me but he wanted your girl Alinna taken care of in return."

"This isn't a favor," Alinna spoke up

"It is when he gave me information on someone I had words with," Dante explained.

"So what are your plans now?" Alinna asked as she stood up and leaned over to look inside Dante chicken box, reaching for a chicken wing.

Looking from his chicken box to Alinna after she boldly took his chicken wing, Dante shook his head, and said, "You have two choices."

"Which are?" Vanessa asked staring hard at Dante. Ignoring Vanessa and her reaching under the table, Dante took another bite of his chicken, and said, "She can either leave Miami or get at this fat fuck."

"You sound like you're going to help us?" Alinna asked staring at Dante,

Holding Alinna's eyes as she finished the rest of the chicken wing, Dante said, "Exactly what kind of help do you want from me?"

"Will you help me?" Alinna asked him. Shaking his head, Dante tossed his chicken breast inside his box then picked up the napkin and wiped his hands. "Look, I'll help out with this shit, but whatever we find we split."

"Deal," Alinna replied smiling across from Dante.

Outside in the KFC parking lot, Dante and Alinna exchanged numbers with each other and then Alinna walked off towards Vanessa truck.

"You're really serious about this aren't you?" Vanessa asked.

"I don't know about this dude, Alinna," Vanessa admitted as she backed out of the parking spot. "First of all, he's a known jack boy, and you know as I do that you can't trust no fucking jack boy. Then why is he even doing this for us ... naw, for you? He don't even know you Alinna."

"I don't know," Alinna admitted as she looked out the window. "But for some reason I believe him," Alinna told Vanessa, speaking Spanish while changing the subject at the same time.

Looking over to Alinna wondering what spicy chicken had to do with what they were talking about, Vanessa quickly realized that Alinna didn't want to talk about Dante and their plans. "Where you wanna get the chicken from Alinna?"

"So you agreed to help shorty? What's the deal fam? When'd you start backing out on your words?" Dante heard Dre ask as he drove home.

"Braw look, you either with me or not, what's up?" Dante asked, heated at Dre for throwing it in his face about him changing his mind.

"Fam, come on, you know I'm with you ain't no doubt, but I'm just surprised you ..."

"Let me hit you back," Dante interrupted checking his line over hearing the line beep from somebody calling in. "Yeah."

"Hey handsome. Had an interesting day, did you?" Recognizing Sergeant Angela Perez's voice from her thick as hell Spanish accent, Dante shook his head and said, "What's up Angela?"

"You tell me, Dante. Who was the girl you left Club Empire with?"

"What girl?"

"Don't play with me Dante, who was she?"

Dante answered, "A friend, Angela."

"What type of friend Dante?"

"Look, what the hell you call me for? I ain't up for 20 questions tonight. Say what the fuck you gotta say."

"I want company tonight. Meet me at the Day's Inn on Columbus Drive."

"I just pulled in front of my apartment ..."

"I expect you at the hotel in twenty minutes, Dante," Angela told him hanging up the phone afterwards.

"Fucking shit," Dante cursed, catching himself before he slung his smart phone across the car only to hear it ring again inside his hand. Looking at the screen this time, surprised to see Alinna calling him so soon, Dante answered, "What's up Alinna?"

"Why you sounding upset? You still mad at me?"

"Naw, I'm good on that. Something else came up. What's up though? You good?"

"Yeah, I'm straight. I was just thinking and I really don't know anything about you."

"I ain't know you were interested in personal background information on me. This some type of interview?"

"I just wanted to know who Dante is. What's your last name for starters?"

"What's yours?"

"Rodriguez," she answered, and asked again, "What's your last name, Dante?"

"You plan on pulling my background up or something?"

40

"Boy, tell me your damn name."

"Blackwell," Dante answered, smiling at her spicy but sexy attitude.

"Dante Blackwell," Alinna repeated, and then asked, "How old are you?"

"Damn nigga, you can't just answer a question straight can you?"

"I'm nineteen," Dante answered with a smirk. "Now you answer the same question, what's your age?"

"Twenty," she answered. "Where are you right now?"

Remembering where he was headed, losing his smile, Dante answered, "I'm headed to handle some business real quick. You home yet?"

"Yeah, I got home a little while ago," Alinna admitted. "So what time are we hooking up tomorrow? I mean for the plan?"

Smirking, Dante said, "Relax shorty. I know what you meant. Just be on standby around noon. I will text you the spot where you're meeting me. Just be quick, this shouldn't take longer than twenty minutes."

"Relax Dante. You're not the only one with a few bodies." Dante smiled at Alinna's comment.

$ $ $

Waking to the feel of lips wrapped around his dick, Dante opened his eyes and lifted his head to find Sergeant Angela Perez's head bobbing up and down between his legs as she tried her best to swallow his dick.

Ultimately fucking the sergeant once again inside her hotel bed, then again in the shower after all of the fucking they did last night, Dante finally got away from the sex-craved bitch, driving away from the Day's Inn.

Pulling out his smartphone, Dante called Big Worm.

"Yeah this is Big Worm. Who is this?"

"Worm, it's me, what's up? I gotta lot to handle today let get this shit over with."

"You take care of that already?"

"Last night, we meeting at her spot?"

"Fuck is we meeting…"

"I left her tied up there last night; just meet me in the parking lot at the apartment by …" Looking at his Casio Mickey Mouse watch, Dante realized that it was nearly noon. "Meet me there by 1:00. That's an hour from now."

"Yeah whatever," Big Worm answered and then abruptly hung up the phone.

Texting while driving, Dante sent the time to Alinna telling her what he wanted her to do, and then he called Dre.

"What up fam?" Dre answered.

"Meet me at Alinna's spot by 12:30. Don't be late and make sure that you have Vegas and Tony T with you."

"I'ma check you then."

"Yeah," Dante answered, hanging up the phone.

Reaching his complex a shortly thereafter, Dante parked at his building in the back of the complex. He shut off the Altima and then hopped out of the car, hit his locks by remote, and jogged inside his apartment building.

Making it to his apartment door, Dante unlocked the front door, and walked inside the two bedroom, one bathroom apartment.

Locking the front door then heading back to his bedroom at the back of the apartment, Dante was already stripping off his clothes.

$ $ $

Seeing the Chevy Avalanche as Dante said she would, Vanessa pulled inside the parking lot. Alinna watched until the Lexus Truck stopped behind the Avalanche then her and both Amber and Harmony climbed out of the Lexus truck.

Closing the passenger door to the Lexus, Alinna walked around the front end of the truck as Vanessa backed the truck out of the parking lot. She saw both the front passenger door and the back door open with two guys climbing out of the Avalanche.

Seeing the muscular guy who she recognized from the previous night and who Dante told her was Dre, Alinna stood as the he walked over to her. "Dre, right?"

"That's what they call me," Dre replied. "Dante told you what's up?"

"It's our idea, so I know what's going on," Alinna cleared up.

Smiling at the attitude, Dre introduced both Vegas and Tony T.

Nodding to both of the guys, Alinna introduced Amber and Harmony.

"What's ya girl's name in the Lexus truck?" Dre asked.

Noticing the smirk on Dre lips, Alinna said while smiling, "Her name is Vanessa, Dre."

"I'm gonna remember that," Dre replied, allowing his smile to show.

$ $ $

Pulling up on his Kawasaki Ninja at exactly 1:00 on the head, Dante turned inside the parking lot at the apartment building that Alinna used as a stash house. He saw Big

Worm's Ford Expedition as well as Dre's Avalanche already parked in the parking lot.

Parking the bike and shutting it off, Dante saw Big Worm climb from the passenger's seat as he climbed off the bike, noticing he brought six friends with him this time.

Dante pulled off his helmet as he walked from the bike, meeting Big Worm and his boy's in the middle of the parking lot. He said, "What's up Worm? You brought more friends with you this time."

"Let's just get this shit over with," Big Worm replied while scanning the parking lot.

Noticing the nervousness from Big Worm as well as the silence from his boys, Dante played it off as if he didn't notice that he led the seven men inside the apartment building and quietly talking to Big Worm as they all headed up the stairwell.

Once at the apartment, Dante pounded twice on the door.

"Who the fuck's all inside there?" Big Wormed asked stepping back from the door.

"Relax fat man, it's my nigga Dre," Dante answered just as the apartment door opened and Dre stood filling the doorway.

"What's up fam?" Dre said to Dante while staring from Big Worm to his boys.

"What up braw?" Dante replied, and then looked back to Big Worm saying, "We doing this or what?"

Sending in his boy's ahead of him, Big Worm followed everyone inside the apartment, shooting Dre a look as he passed him while entering the apartment.

"This is what you wanted, right?" Big Worm heard Dante say as he was entering the front room of the apartment.

Slowly smiling at seeing Alinna tied to a chair with her mouth gagged.

"Now this is what the fuck I'm talking about," Big Worm said, smiling as he walked through his boys to the front to stand in front of Alinna, seeing the answer in her eyes as she starred up at him. "That's exactly how I like to see you, bitch. You ain't talking that gangster shit now. And where the fuck is your hero bitch Vanessa at now?"

Slapping Alinna across the face, Big Worm eye's opened wide as he watched Alinna's hands swing from around her back and the rope that was around her fall free. "What the fuck?"

"Now you fat motherfucker, what were you just saying?" Vanessa spoke up, causing Big Worm and his boys to all turn around looking back behind them.

Seeing Vanessa, Amber, and Harmony along with Dre and two other guys, each of which with guns in their hands,

46

Big Worm turned and looked at Dante only to look back behind him and hearing, "You looking for me fat boy?"

"Ww ... what the hell is ..."

Swinging and connecting with Big Worm's face, Alinna continued swinging and beating the shit out of Big Worm who screamed like a bitch as he lay balled up on the ground.

Smirking as he leaned against the wall, watching Alinna stomp and kick the shit out of Big Worm, Dante shifted his eyes over to one of the six guys he remembered from the last time he met up with Big Worm, calling out to get his attention then nodding him over.

"I'm not going to make this long. You got two choices. One is you can agree to show me where the money and work is; or two, I'll end what life you got right now. Choose now," Dante told the guy, sliding one of his hammers from the front of his jeans.

Seeing the guy nod his head in agreement, Dante smiled a small smile saying, "Smart man, real smart man."

5

Once Alinna tired herself out from beating the shit out of Big Worm, Dante had Dre take care of that fat motherfucker while the others dealt with the rest of Big Worm's crew, grabbing the one who agreed to show him where the money was stashed. Taking Dre's Avalanche, both Dante and Alinna left together with Big Worm's man.

"Where we going, Dante?" Alinna asked, as she watched the guy walking out in front of her and Dante.

"Our new friend here agreed to take us to Big Worm's stash spot and trap house," Dante said as they headed down stairs and out to the parking lot.

Once at the Avalanche, Dante first grabbed homeboy and patted him down, removing the 9MM Beretta from inside his back pocket. Handing it to Alinna, he then put homeboy inside the Avalanche.

"What do you plan on doing with him once you get the money and the work?" Alinna asked Dante outside the Avalanche.

"I'll let you decide that," Dante told her as he walked to the driver's side.

After leaving the apartment and following homeboy's directions, Dante pulled up to a house that was easily recognizable as a trap house. Four guys were posted out on the front porch with thick smoke in the air as they each started out at the Avalanche.

"Get out," Dante instructed Big Worm's man. "Play stupid and I promise you will lay dead with the rest of them. Now get out."

Both the guy and Alinna climbed out from the passenger side as Dante walked around the Avalanche seeing Alinna standing close up on the guy.

"Let's get this over with quickly."

Following homeboy inside the yard and up towards the front porch where the four guy's now stood staring at them, Dante shifted his eye's to the dark skin guy who spoke first. "Crig, who is this you bought with you? Where is Big Worm?"

"Big Worm sent me to pick…"

"Who the fuck is this nigga and the bitch you…"

Boom! Boom! Boom! Boom!

Tired of the talking and time wasting, Dante snatched his .40 from under his shirt in the front of his jeans, and before anyone knew what was happening, he dropped all four guys on the front porch.

"Let's go," Dante told him, pushing him forwards but tossing the keys to the Avalanche to Alinna saying, "Have the truck ready."

Watching Dante follow the guy up onto the porch seeing Dante shoot two guys that laid on the porch as he passed them entering into the house. Alinna shook her head and then turned, heading back out to the Avalanche.

$ $ $

Leaving Big Worm's trap house after Dante and Big Worm's man spent less than five minutes inside, Alinna pulled the Avalanche in front of another house that was located in a better neighborhood.

Once Dante followed the guy inside the house, Alinna counted to three before she heard the shooting from inside the house. After nearly five minutes of gunshots, both Dante and the guy came out of the house. Dante pushed the guy toward the truck while holding a black duffel bag on this right shoulder.

Pulling off as soon as the both of them were inside the back of the Avalanche, Alinna looked back at Dante through the rearview mirror catching his eyes.

"What now?"

"You come up with a decision yet about what I asked you to decide?" Dante asked her.

Shifting her eye's over to the guy sitting beside Dante as he sat staring back at her, Alinna focused back on the road saying, "What use do have for him?"

"Then pull over up ahead and let him out," Dante told Alinna and nodding his head.

Doing as Dante instructed, Alinna pulled the Avalanche over at the side of the street, then looked back as Dante opened the back door and got out, instructing the guy to get out.

Watching as the guy got out the back of the Avalanche, Alinna almost missed the movement because it was so fast. She caught Dante grabbing the guy's shirtfront swinging him out towards the street, and in the same motion, pointing the glock at the guys face and pulling the trigger. *Boom!*

Climbing in the front seat after calmly closing the backdoor, Dante closed the passenger door while noticing the way Alinna stared at him. "You may wanna drive."

Doing as she was told, Alinna pulled off and glanced at the rearview mirror seeing the body laid out in the middle of the street where Dante left it.

"What's your plan's now, shorty?" Dante spoke up asking after few minutes.

Shaking her head, Alinna looked over to Dante but then focused back on the road saying, "One small problem gone, but now I still need to deal with an even a bigger problem."

"What's the bigger problem?" Dante asked before he realized what he was doing.

"It's nothing. I'm going to figure it out," Alinna told him as she looked over seeing Dante pulling out a box of Black and Mild's from his pocket.

After a quiet moment while lighting up one of his Black's, Dante gave in and asked, "What's the problem Alinna?"

Looking over to Dante a moment, Alinna turned back to the road and said, "I'm having problems finding a new connect."

"What up with the one you're using now?" Dante asked. Watching as she shook her head, Alinna told him about the bullshit that she was going through with Kenny K, and how she wanted to get away from him to find a better contact but was having a hard time finding one that would deal with a female on a serious level.

"So what're you planning now?" Dante asked once Alinna finished speaking.

"This guy I know is supposed to be setting up a meeting to get me introduced to this guy named Geovani out in ..."

"Atlanta," Dante finished for her sentence. "I've heard of him."

"I see you get around," Alinna told Dante smiling at him.

"Tell me about this Kenny K dude," Dante told her without responding to her previous statement.

"What are you plotting, Dante?" Alinna asked while staring at Dante. "Don't go doing nothing stupid. I still gotta get my work from this guy."

"Just tell me about the clown," Dante told her, raising the black up to his lips, pulling on the plastic tip, feeling the smooth flavor cigar smoke flow fill his mouth.

$ $ $

Once they returned to the apartment, they headed up the stairs carrying two gym bags while Alinna carried the duffle bag that came from the stash house. Dante followed alongside Alinna as she led the way to the apartment door.

Hearing the laughter as soon as Alinna got to the front door open of the apartment, Dante followed Alinna inside just as Dre came walking from the front room to meet them.

"What's up fam? Everything good?" Dre asked Dante, seeing both the bags Dante and Alinna were holding.

"Everything good braw?" Dante answered as Vanessa walked up to Alinna questioning her girl, but catching the look the amazon shot his way.

Inside the front room where the others already were, both Alinna and Dante found themselves seated side by side on the sofa as the others stood around or sat on the two couches on either side of them.

Emptying both gym bags and then the duffel bag onto the wooden coffee table in front of them, both Alinna and Dante separated the money from the weed and coke.

After totaling $20,000 from the stash house and $3,000 from the trap house, Dante allowed Alinna and Vanessa to count out what the weed and coke came back to.

"It's two whole bricks of coke and three quarters of a brick as well as two pounds of weed," Alinna told the others, but looked to Dante as she said it.

"So is that what you said; $23,000 to split between the eight of us?" Dante asked meeting Alinna's eyes.

"Hold up," Vegas spoke up drawing every ones attention to him. "You say $23,000 split eight ways?"

"That's right, that's what … A little under four thousand for each of us," Tony T commented staring at Dante.

"Dee, come on dawg. You called us to help these chicks to get paid eight stacks?" Vegas asked him. "We must be getting some kind of work?"

"First of all nigga, we didn't ask for you or your punk-ass homeboys help," Vanessa spoke up and was about to continue when Dante interrupted.

"You'll shut up a second."

"Man, I know we're not …"

"Vegas, what the fuck did I just say?" Dante asked, looking over to his crying-ass homeboy.

"Whatever man," Vegas said raising up both his hands in surrender.

Running towards Dre and motioning him over, Dante whispered into Dre's ear receiving a nod in agreement and then looking at Vegas and Tony T. "To make you niggas happy, you two got mine and Dre's cut, that's $8,000 apiece. If that's not good enough, then we may have a problem."

"That's straight with me," Tony T spoke up.

"Whatever Dee, my nigga," Vegas said, shaking his head as he stared at Dante.

"Smart," Dante replied and then looked over to Alinna saying, "Give these two eight grand a piece."

"Vanessa, give them the money," Alinna told her girl and then turned back to Dante grabbing his arm and pulling him up as she stood up from the sofa.

"Come with me; we need to talk."

Allowing Alinna to lead him from the front room into the open bedroom door that was completely empty, Dante turned facing her as she stepped around him closing the bedroom door.

"Dante, what the hell are you doing?" Alinna started off with much attitude. "Why the hell would you agree to give those two half of your money? That don't make any damn sense."

"Shorty relax for a ..."

"Don't tell me to fucking relax," she cut Dante off and then shoved him in the chest.

"What type of homeboy's are they if they cut you out like that?"

"They're more business friends then any kind of friends," Dante told her smirking. "Don't get me wrong, we all hang out and get money together, but it's really Dre that's more like my brother. We do our thing together. Every once in a while we all hook up for a major hit if one comes up where me and Dre need backup, which isn't often."

"So you just wanna give their asses your money?" Alinna asked, placing her hands on her curvy and spread hips.

"I'm plotting on something bigger," Dante admitted but then added. "But I wanna holla at you about this idea that I been thinking about, you wanna listen or what?"

Staring up at Dante holding his eyes a moment, Alinna sucked her teeth as she folded her arms across her chest. "This shit better be worth me listening."

$ $ $

Walking back out into the front room after they finished talking, Alinna noticed both Tony T and Vegas were gone and Dre was standing outside on the balcony talking on his cell phone.

Nodding her head at Dante, motioning that he was going out to talk to Dre, Alinna walked back over to the soft couch and sat down beside Vanessa only to hear Amber ask, "Hey, what's going on? Why are you pulling pretty boy gangster off to the side like that instead of just talking in front of us?"

"I'm about to explain that now," Alinna looked from Amber to Harmony to Vanessa. "I need y'all to really hear me out and think about what I'm about to tell y'all because what me and Dante just finished discussing. If we all agree to this it just may help solve all of our problems."

"What the hell are you talking about, Alinna?" Vanessa asked staring at Alinna with a what-the-hell's-going-on stare.

6

Seeing the same clowns as before when they came to pick up their re-up package from Kenny K's ass at the same trap house, only this time to see Kenny K outside with his clowns, Alinna waited until Vanessa parked the Lexus Truck, then they both climbed out.

Walking around the back end of the truck just as Vanessa was closing the driver's door, Alinna saw the surprised look on Kenny K's face as she and Vanessa entered the front gate.

"What the fuck are you two doing here?" Kenny K asked turning towards both Alinna and Vanessa as she stood on the porch with his face balled up. "I don't remember telling you or this he-she bitch to come around my spot."

"Kenny K, look," Alinna told him ignoring the way he was talking to them. "We're here to tell you that it's over. We're done fucking with you and dealing with your bullshit."

"Bitch, what'd you say?" Kenny K barked at Alinna stepping off the porch. Walking up to Alinna. "Bitch, who the fuck do you think you talking to?"

"You heard what the fuck I said, Kenny K," Alinna told him, staring hard inside of his eyes.

"Bitch, you must have forgot ..." Stopping confused, he watched as his boys were shot dead, and looking to the right only to see a large guy holding an AR-15 who was the cause of his boy's being chopped up like Swiss cheese.

Feeling the recognizable feeling of a gun at the back of his head, Kenny K froze and heard, "Turn your punk ass around, nigga."

Doing as he was ordered, Kenny K slowly turned around only to face off with a light brown-skinned guy he never saw before. "Man who the fuck are you? I ain't got no ..."

Kicking out forward and connecting his boots into Kenny K mid-section, knocking him down to his knees, Dante lowered his burner aiming it at Kenny K as Alinna stepped up beside him.

"You were saying something, nigga?" Alinna asked smiling a nasty smile down at Kenny K as he kneeled, looking at her while trying to catch his breath. "I told you before shit was gonna change. Now look at your soft ass."

Seeing Dre walk back out of the trap house carrying three backpacks, Alinna looked over to Vanessa, and then towards Dre then focused back on Kenny K. "It's been nice talking with you, but I gotta go now."

Turning away and staring back towards the Lexus truck after seeing both Dre and Vanessa jogging off around the trap house together, Alinna heard Dante's Glock ring out once, twice, and then twice more by the time she stopped at the driver's door to the truck.

"I'm driving," Dante told Alinna as he jogged up beside her at the driver's door holding up the truck keys Vanessa tossed him as she and Dre took off.

Getting inside the Lexus and cranking it up by the time Alinna walked around to the passenger side and was climbing inside the truck, Dante smashed out from in front of the trap house. They flew up the street and took a right at the corner fish tailing the truck.

"You know you should really be a motivation speaker," Dante told Alinna glancing over to her. "All that talking you were doing to those cowards. Fuck all that. We've been planning this shit for four days and you stood talking like a clown for seemingly four years."

Playfully punching Dante in the arm, she smiled over at him and rolled her eyes as she reached for the half-smoked joint that was inside the ashtray. "How the hell did you and Dre get around the back of the house so fast?"

"We're hood-niggas's, shorty," Dante answered smiling over at Alinna. "We jumped the back gate and ran around the side of the house while you was still talking, running your damn mouth."

"Fuck you, Dante," Alinna told him, blowing thick hydro weed smoke. "You and Dre still hitting Rico across town tomorrow?"

"Pretty much," Dante answered just as his cell phone went off, and then seconds later Alinna's phone went off.

Pulling out his cell phone, Dante looked to the screen only to see Angela calling. "Shit."

Looking over to Dante hearing him as she pulled her iPhone from her pocket, Alinna shook her head at Dante with a mixed attitude. She looked at her cell phone screen and saw that it was Miguel calling. "Yeah Miguel, what's up?"

"What's up my heart, where are you?"

"Driving, why?"

"I have my friend here I told you about. He's ready to meet you."

Smiling at the news, Alinna asked, "When does he want to meet?"

"Now," Miguel answered. "How soon can you be at the Starbucks on 82nd and 21st Avenue?"

"Gimme twenty minutes."

"You got fifteen," Miguel told her, and then hung up the phone.

Ignoring him hanging up on her, Alinna looked to Dante to tell him the good news only to see his balled up face and the way his right hand was gripping the steering wheel. "Dante what's wrong? What happened?"

"Nothing, I'm good," Dante answered, staring straight ahead as he drove.

Wanting to push him into telling her what was wrong with him but decided against it, Alinna figured he would tell her if he wanted her to know but instead said, "Guess what? You remember I told you about the friend I know that supposed to introduce me to Geovani guy?"

"Yeah I remember, what about him?"

"He wants to meet right now."

Looking over to Alinna, seeing her smile Dante looked away and asked, "Where at?"

"Starbucks off of 82nd and 21st," Alinna told him. "You gonna go with me, right?"

Glancing over back to Alinna, Dante said, "Fuck it," in his head deciding Alinna over Angela, turning the Lexus truck around heading back in the other direction, and catching the smile Alinna shot him.

$ $ $

Pulling inside the Starbucks parking lot fifteen minutes later, Dante found an open parking spot then both he and Alinna climbed out of the truck.

Heading towards the front entrance just as the door swung open, Alinna saw Miguel walk out of the Starbucks with a huge smile on his face as he headed directly at her.

"My sweetie…"

Upon seeing Dante when he stepped over the front of her just as Miguel walked directly into him, Alinna never had the chance to say anything and never would have. Dante kicked out Miguel's left leg as he grabbed and twisted his left arm behind his back as Miguel dropped to his left knee.

"What the fuck!" Miguel yelled in pain, reaching for his right side arm at his only to feel the barrel of a gun pressed to the side of his head.

"Dante, it's alright," Alinna spoke up with a small smile on her lips. "This the friend I told you about."

Dante released Alinna's heavyset Spanish friend who slowly stood to his feet and rubbed his arm while staring at him. Dante stuck his burner back inside the front of his jeans as Miguel spoke directly to Alinna. "You called this guy, Dante? As in the same Dante who has half the drug dealers in the city scared shitless?"

Nodding her head still smiling, Alinna introduced the two. "Sergeant Miguel Ruiz, meet my boyfriend Dante."

"Your boy…" Miguel stated, looking from Alinna to Dante then back to Alinna. "But you sell drugs and he's a jack boy. How can …"

"Aren't we here to meet someone about business or were there other reasons we drove way out here?" Dante asked, cutting Miguel off.

Staring at Dante briefly and slowly shaking his head, Miguel looked over to Alinna and shook his head again as he turned and began walking back towards the coffee shop entrance.

"Your boyfriend, huh?" Dante asked, looking over to Alinna as they followed behind Miguel.

"Don't read too much into it," Alinna told him, smirking at Dante as she stepped inside the Starbucks behind Miguel with Dante following behind her.

Following Miguel over to the table at the back corner of the Starbucks where a young Spanish man sat talking on a cell phone, Alinna stood beside Miguel in front of the guy's table noticing Miguel walking around with a confused look upon his face.

"You must be Rodriguez?" the guy spoke up, laying his cell phone down onto the tables standing up.

"And you are?" Alinna asked, taking the guy's hand and shaking it.

"Mario Sanchez, meet Alinna Rodriguez," Miguel introduced, finally getting into the conversation.

"You're not what I expected," Mario told her, pulling out a chair for her as he slowly looked her over with a small smile.

"I'm not sure what you were expecting," Alinna replied as she sat down in the seat that was offered to her. Ignoring the way Sanchez was looking her.

"I'm just really surprised at how beautiful you are."

"Sanchez, look kid," Miguel interrupted getting Mario's attention. "Let's just stick to business. You really don't want to go there with Alinna, trust my words on that."

Looking back to Alinna and seeing the small smile on her sexy pouty full lips, Mario decided to wait his time out and changing the subject by saying, "So you're looking to connect with Mr. Geovani are you?"

"I'll be honest with you, Ms. Rodriguez; this type of business isn't really a business for a woman. Don't get me wrong, I'm not saying that you're not able to handle yourself, but what I am saying is that Mr. Geovani is very … how can I put this? Mr. Geovani does not trust his time or his business with just any and every one."

"So basically what you're telling me is that me doing some begging for you for Mr. Geovani to even consider having a sit down with you," Mario explained and then gave a smirk while adding, "However, I am willing to do what I must for your Ms. Rodriguez. But what am I to receive for my hard work and time?"

"Sanchez don't …"

"What exactly are you looking for in return?" Dante asked, as he appeared next to Mario at the table.

"What the hell?" Mario asked, hopping up from this seat only to have Dante forcefully shove him back down in the seat. "Who the fuck is this guy? What the hell is going on?"

"I tried to warn you kid," Miguel said, shaking his head at Mario with a look on his face. "This is the reason why I told you to stick to business, kid."

"Who the fuck is this guy?" Mario asked again looking up at the guy that was standing over him.

"Mario allow me to introduce you to my business partner and boyfriend, Dante Blackwell," Alinna smiled at seeing the expression on Mario face.

Pulling a chair over from the table next to them Dante turned the seat backwards sitting down, he asked, "So can we get business done or not? Straight answer - yes or no?"

"I'm not sure ..."

"Yes or no?" Dante interrupted staring hard at Mario.

Slowly nodding his head while staring back at Dante, Mario answered, "Yeah, yes I can get the meeting set up."

"Good," Alinna spoke up, smiling from across the table at Mario.

$ $ $

"How the hell did you get mixed up with this guy, Alinna? What the hell?" Miguel said as they stood outside the Starbucks parking lot follow their meeting with Mario.

"Miguel, I'm not about to explain to you who I'm dealing with – business or personally, just make sure you stay on Mario and this meeting," Alinna told Miguel before turning to leave only for Miguel to grab her arm stopping her.

Quickly releasing her after realizing what the hell he was doing, Miguel looked up only to see what he expected. He reached for his side arm only a few seconds to late. Dante's two Glocks seemed to fly from his waistband and into his hands just as Dante walked up behind Alinna.

"Miguel, just handle what I asked you to handle please," Alinna told him. Staring at Miguel a moment but then turned away saying as she walked around Dante, "Dante, let's go."

Sliding both of his burners back into his waist of his jeans and staring hard at Miguel, Dante turned his back and followed Alinna back to her truck.

Back behind the wheel after letting Alinna inside, Dante started the truck and backed out of the parking spot, asking, "How the hell did you hooked up with that dude?"

"It's a long story," Alinna answered but added don't pay Miguel any attention.

"I don't like or trust that dude."

"You don't like or trust anyone, Dante."

"I trust you," Dante replied looking from the road over to Alinna.

Meeting his eyes, Alinna stared until Dante focused back on the road, she asked, "What do you think of the meeting with Mario?"

"I don't trust him."

Smiling a devious smile as he cut his eyes over to Alinna, Dante asked, "So you're letting me and Dre at this dude?"

"That was our agreement right?" Alinna said smiling back at Dante winking her eye at him.

Nodding his head and smiling harder, Dante focused back on the road already thinking ahead about what they may come up with from this Geovani hit.

$ $ $

Making it to Alinna's townhouse ten minutes later after stopping at the gas station, picking up gas, and Alinna buying a box of blunt wrap's for herself and a box of Vanilla and Mild's, Dante parked the truck besides Dre's Avalanche then he and Alinna climbed from the truck.

Heading up to the front door, Alinna unlocked and opened it. She led Dante inside just in time to see Vanessa. A few minutes later, Dre stumbled down the stairs.

Seeing Vanessa's hair messed up and her jeans opened in front while Dre's shirt was half on and his jeans also open in the front, Alinna looked back at Dante smiling at Dante who was also smirking.

"You want something to drink, Dante?" Alinna asked him, smiling still as she headed for the kitchen.

"What you got shorty?" Dante asked, shaking his head at Dre and Vanessa again as he followed behind Alinna.

"Yo fam, let me holla at you," Dre called out following Dante from behind.

"Alinna, I can explain," Vanessa told her girl as she grabbed two bottles of Corona from the refrigerator.

Taking the beer from Alinna, Dante looked to Dre and asked, "What came back from the hit, braw?"

"That is if you two got around to checking it," Alinna added jokingly.

Laughing at seeing the look on both Dre and Vanessa's faces as he and Alinna headed to the den, Dante said, "Braw, just get the stuff and bring it to the den."

Looking to Vanessa as she looked at him, Dante asked, "So what now?"

"Just come on Andre," Vanessa told him, grabbing the front of Dre shirt leading him back upstairs.

Once both Dre and Vanessa got the three backpacks and met them in the den, Dante and Alinna went through the bags together.

"I called Amber and Harmony. They should be here soon," Vanessa spoke up from beside Dre.

Hearing Vanessa but not responding, Alinna looked at Dre seeing him counting small bills from one of the three backpacks. "It's about two bricks of coke and a pound of weed, but one of the bricks is already broken down in ounces and twenty's even ten's and five dollar stacks."

Nodding his head in understanding but continuing to count the money, Dante paid no attention to the knocking at the front door.

"What's up y'all?" Amber asked a few minutes later after Vanessa went to answer the front door, walking into the den with the others.

"Where's Harmony?" Alinna asked Amber, looking from Dante.

"I don't know, she called me and said she was taking care of something. She should be here soon I guess," Amber answered, looking at the weed and coke on the glass coffee table, plus the money Dante was counting.

"Y'all did the hit?"

"There's $11,000 and some change here," Dante told the group as soon as he finish counting.

Nodding her head, Alinna said, "Alright y'all, I'll tell Harmony later. Y'all listen up, Dante and I just met with the Geovani guy. A meeting is being set up with Geovani and us."

7

After the first meeting with Geovani that was made possible by Mario, Vanessa and Alinna met up with the middle aged, well-groomed Spanish drug dealer.

Agreeing on four and a half bricks and five pounds of weed after the three-hour meeting, Alinna and Vanessa shook hands with Geovani, and then shook hands with Mario.

Once inside Alinna's Lexus I.S. 350, with Vanessa behind the wheel driving away from the agreed meeting spot in Atlanta, Alinna called Dante phone. "Yeah shorty."

"Where are you?"

"Look to your left."

Doing as she was told, she looked towards Vanessa, but focused on the driver's side window just as the rental Ford Explorer drove up beside them, seeing Dante inside the passenger seat next to Dre who was driving.

"How'd everything go?" Dante asked, staring across at Alinna, speaking into the cell phone.

"Everything went good," Alinna said into the cell watching the Explorer pull off from beside the Lexus. "The buy is set for the day after tomorrow."

"Big security?"

"Six guy's with him, but two more that stood outside the restaurant with the limo that Geovani pulled up in."

"Alright, we'll talk back at the hotel," Dante told her, hanging up the phone.

"What'd he say?" Vanessa asked as soon as she saw Alinna lowered the phone from her ear.

"You know how Dante is. He didn't say too much of anything," Alinna told Vanessa, shaking her head as she stared at the Explorer.

"You think they will really be able to pull this off, Alinna?" Vanessa asked. "I mean it's just the two of them and we didn't even bring Amber and Harmony for back up for them."

"I don't know why but I think they'll be okay. Dante actually looks as if he's enjoying all this,"

"But this is not one of those small time dudes like back in Miami. This dude Geovani seems like he's about his issues, Alinna."

Looking over to Vanessa, Alinna gave a small smile saying, "Don't let me find out that you're actually getting soft on me, Vanessa, or is it that you're worried about your new man, Dre – or should I say Andre as you call him?"

Rolling her eyes at Alinna causing her girl to bust out laughing, Vanessa waited until Alinna stopped laughing then said, "I was just asking because whether you remember or not we're putting everything on these two and if they fuck up we fucked up to Alinna."

Growing serious, Alinna looked to Vanessa and said, "I'm fully aware what's being put up with Dante and Dre coming through for us but I can't explain it. I trust Dante, and Dre is his boy so I trust him too. We'll be straight."

Looking to Alinna and seeing the expression on her girls face, Vanessa began saying something, but decided against it. She simply smiled as she turned her focus back to the road.

$ $ $

Once back at the hotel, the four of them headed to Vanessa and Alinna's room. Dante positioned himself against the wall next to the dresser in front of the bed smoking a Black, while Dre sat on the hotel room couch with Vanessa sitting on his lap while Alinna sat on the hotel room's queen size bed, telling both Dante and Dre about the meeting with Geovani. Vanessa added in helping Alinna out.

"So this Geovani guy wasn't acting nervous or worried through the whole meeting?" Dante asked Alinna once she finished talking.

"He did at first," Vanessa answered. "When he first showed up he was watchful, carefully inspecting everything. But after he saw that it was just two females by themselves he relaxed and actually laughed a little."

"When is the buy supposed to go down?" Dante asked, even though Alinna had told him once before.

"He wants to have it done the day after tomorrow," Alinna answered staring at Dante watching him as he leaned against the wall deep in though.

"Alright," Dante finally spoke up after a moment.

"Where's the pick up going to be? Same place or someplace different?"

"We got him to agree to set up the buy and pick up at a rest stop off I-95," Alinna told him with a smirk.

Dante said, "I think I'm falling in love with you, shorty."

"So what's your plan?" Alinna asked Dante as he was walking out of the bathroom, seeing him stretched out on the couch. She noticed both Vanessa and Dre were missing.

"I haven't decided yet," Dante answered as Alinna walked over to the couch, pushing his feet off of the couch arm so she could sit down beside him.

"Where's Nessa and Dre?" Alinna asked him.

"You really want to know?" Dante asked smiling a small smirk and cutting his eyes back over to Alinna.

"Not really," Alinna answered as she smiled at Dre but really just noticing how cut he was. "You should smile more. It really make you look cuter."

"Cuter, huh?"

Ignoring the way Dante was staring at her, she asked him, "I've never see you with girls even though I see them trying to get your attention. Do you have a girl, Dante?"

"You asking because ..." Dante asked staring at Alinna.

"Why can't you ever answer a question without asking one first?"

"You ever just get straight to the point without asking 20 questions?"

Sucking her teeth, she pushed Dante's leg as she jumped up from the beside of him on the couch, Alinna stomped off only to stop when she felt herself lifted off her feet, screaming as she began twisting and turning, fighting to get out of Dante arm's. "Put me the fuck down, Dante!"

Ignoring Alinna as he walked over to the queen size bed and tossing Alinna onto the bed causing her to bounce, Dante snatched off his shirt then began undoing his jeans while kicking off his Timbs.

"What the hell you think you doing?" Alinna asked, looking over to the night table where Dante was sitting both .40's.

"Take that shit off or I'm gonna take it off for you," Dante instructed Alinna, as he stepped out of his jeans.

"Fuck you!" Alinna told him, but hurried off the bed when Dante grabbed the back of her jeans. "Aaahhh!"

Ignoring Alinna's screaming and scraping at him as well as the blow's she threw at him, Dante simply ripped the shirt she was wearing off her back, and then began to undo her jeans as she fought him the entire time he worked.

Fighting Dante in her thong and a Gucci shirt that he ripped open, Alinna punched and scratched at him but stop dead in mid-swing with her eyes and mouth wide open after feeling the size of him as he slowly slid in her.

Feeling exactly when Alinna stopped fighting, Dante smiled as he lifted up above her, meeting her eyes while slowly moving in and out of her.

"Now tell me now the reason why you were questioning me about having a girl."

Opening her mouth to speak but unable to form words, Alinna simply released a deep moan as she reached for Dante.

Allowing Alinna to pull him down against her, feeling her pushing up meeting him as he went deep inside her, Dante turned his lips to her ear first kissing her ear loaf, licking it then whispering, "This what you wanted isn't it?"

Nodding her head, Alinna gripped Dante back tighter as he pushed deeper inside her causing a scream to rip from her throat.

"When I ask a question, you answer me with words. Do we understand each other?" Dante told her speaking into Alinna ear again.

"Yesss, yes Dante, yess," she moaned for him.

"Now isn't this what you wanted or is it something more you want?" he asked as he ran his right hand up to her right breast pulling the bra cup down feeling her breast.

Feeling herself close to cumming, Alinna moaned out, "Dante, Dante I'm ... I'm getting ready to cum."

"Then you better tell me what I want to hear or I'm gonna stop that nut from popping," Dante told her pumping deeper as a little deeper as he played with her right pink nipple. "Talk shorty or I'm stopping."

"Dante pleeeasses," Alinna cried, feeling herself close to cumming.

"Last chance; talk Alinna," Dante ordered, slowing down only to have Alinna legs wrapped around his waist trying to force him deeper inside of her. "Talk Alinna."

"It's you Dante. I want you nigga. I want your stupid ass, now make me cum damn it," Alinna screamed, beating his back.

"My pleasure," Dante replied, smiling as he began digging deeper and slamming inside of Alinna causing her to scream at the top of her lungs as she exploded hard with enough pressure he felt her squirting back at him from her pussy.

$ $ $

Vanessa woke Dante up the next morning with her loud laughter and then walked into the room, picked up Dante's jeans in her left hand, and Alinna's ripped panties in her right. Dante laid with a smile on his lips while Alinna curled up under him pulling the blanket up over her head.

"Vanessa, get the hell out of here and take Dre with you!" Alinna yelled from under the blanket.

"I may as well get something to wear and go back to Andre's room," Vanessa said, still smiling as she went over to her recently purchased bag.

Waiting until both Dre and Vanessa finally left the room, Dante pulled the blanket from over Alinna's head. "They're gone, shorty."

"I can't believe I was sleeping that hard," Alinna said sitting up in bed. "How did we let them walk in on us still sleeping together?"

"Whoa hold up, shorty," Dante said losing his smile as he sat upwards. "What do you mean catching us sleeping together? You trying to make this shit some type of secret between us?"

"Dante, that's not what I'm ..."

"You know what, I'm tripping," Dante said throwing the blanket off and climbing out of bed.

"Dante what are you doing?" Alinna called to him watching him grab up his clothes.

Ignoring Alinna after feeling like a straight sucker, Dante headed towards the bathroom only for Alinna to rush up behind him pushing him through the doorway in the bathroom.

"Nigga, don't walk away from me. I'm talking to yo ass," Alinna said angrily staring at Dante as he stood staring angrily back at her.

Not even bothering with responding, Dante simply tossed his clothes onto the sink counter then walked over towards the standing shower.

Rushing over to Dante and pushing him away from the shower door to block the shower, Alinna said, "Dante I'm telling you now boy, I ain't scared of your ass. I will fuck you up if you don't stop ignoring me. I hate that shit."

"Move Alinna," Dante commanded.

"Fuck you," she replied.

Walking up on her, he picked her up in his left arm ignoring her as she hit him while opening the shower door; he carried Alinna into the shower with him.

"Put me down, Dante," Alinna demanded.

Putting her down and then turning his back to her facing the showerhead, Dante turned on the shower still ignoring her.

Taking a deep breath and blowing it out, Alina said, "Dante look, alright I made a mistake with the words I used. I was just surprised when they walked in on us, but you know from last night that I want you, and if you want me to tell Vanessa or whoever else, I will. Will you please talk to me?"

Turning facing Alinna, Dante stared at her for a moment wondering if it was her or him, not understanding why he allowed himself to become emotional over and about this chick. Wondering if he was even able to control the way he reacted to her or about her.

Noticing and recognizing the deep thoughts and expression on Dante's face that he always got when he thought hard about something, Alinna stepped closer against him reaching up and touching Dante on the right side of his face seeing, she broke his concentration. "Dante, are we going to fight our first day together, or can we do something like what we did last night?"

Shaking his head, Dante gripped her around the waist and lifted her up from her feet as she wrapped her legs around his waist.

"How did you know I wanted you?" Alinna asked as she realized and reached between them, gripping Dante manhood.

"Because we're a lot alike," Dante told her as Alinna lead him inside of her, listening as she moaned his name. He gripped her soft, phat but firm ass saying as he closed his eyes, "You gonna be the death of me."

"I'm gonna be the life of you," Alinna told him, wrapping both of her arms around his neck as Dante lifted and then lowered her onto his manhood.

8

Getting to sleep early after shopping and hanging out with Vanessa and without seeing Dante or Dre after leaving the hotel for something to eat yesterday morning, Alinna woke up to find Dante's side of the bed empty after falling asleep next to him the previous night.

Ignoring the vacant feeling, Alinna climbed out from the bed. She dragged herself to the bathroom to use the toilet and take a quick shower before the set time to meet with Geovani for the buy and pick.

Nearly five minutes passed inside the shower when she heard Vanessa yell out to her from the room. Alinna finished with her shower and even washing her hair with cheap hotel shampoo.

After finishing with her shower, drying off, and wrapping her towel around her at breast level with the towel reaching her mid-thigh level, Alinna left the bathroom, walking back out into the room seeing Vanessa seated on the bed in only her panties and bra talking on the phone. "That's Dre you're talking too?"

"Harmony," Vanessa answered, moving the phone from her lips then putting it back after she said it listening to what Harmony was telling her.

Putting on black silk boy shorts, Dante said that he liked what she bought yesterday along with the matching bra.

Alinna was pulling out a Gucci skirt outfit when Vanessa called to her.

"What's up Vanessa?" Alinna said, looking over to her girl.

"You're not gonna believe what I just heard. We're going to have a problem once we get back to Miami."

"What's going on?"

"Harmony just told me that Tony T was shot last night and is in the hospital. He won't tell her what happened but this is what you not going to believe," Vanessa told her while smiling at Alinna. "She and Tony T are kicking it with each other."

She stared at Vanessa in surprise both at what she just heard about what happened to Tony T and that they were a couple. Alinna shook her head saying, "Dante and Dre are going to really trip about their boy once they find out. "How's he doing?"

"He's doing okay, he got hit twice. Once in the left leg and another in the right upper chest," Harmony said. "He's doing okay though," Vanessa told Alinna and then said, "You're not going to believe how she really found out about Tony T."

Shaking her head, Alinna understood why Harmony was always missing in action or late showing up. "Let's get ready girl. We gotta get to the place to meet up with Geovani and his people."

"Did you talk to Dante?" Vanessa asked as she stood up from the bed heading towards the bathroom.

"He won't talk," Alinna answered. "He just told me last night to be ready to handle business."

"At least he told you that much. Andre's ass ain't tell me shit with his fat head ass," Vanessa said, slamming the bathroom door closed.

$ $ $

Leaving the hotel after checking out, Vanessa drove the Lexus IS360 while Alinna sat in the passenger side looking through the Burberry backpack that carried $30,000 that showed once the bag was open. Cut green copy paper was at the bottom of the bag, which looked as if it was wrapped stacks of bills.

Once they reached the rest stop a few minutes later, Alinna found herself looking around, seeing if she could spot Dante or Dre anywhere.

"You may as well stop looking. You know you'll never find either one of their asses," Alinna heard Vanessa say, but continued to look around anyway.

Once they parked and waited nearly 10 minutes, a black Benz truck and two black suburban's drove in the parking lot of the rest stop. Both Alinna and Vanessa climbed from the Lexus.

Handing Vanessa the backpack as they walked, they headed towards the three S.U.V.'s. Alinna saw at least ten armed men climb out of one suburban only to see ten more climb from the second suburban.

"Damn," Vanessa said under her breath at also seeing how many men climbed from both trucks.

Hearing and ignoring Vanessa who was staring at the back door to the Benz truck, the driver climbed from the Benz also armed, opening the backdoor. Alinna saw Geovani and Mario climb from the back of the Benz truck.

"Good morning, ladies," Geovani said, smirking as both Vanessa and Alinna walked up.

"Good morning, Mr. Geovani," Alinna replied, and then asked, "Is everything ready?"

Nodding his head, Geovani shifted his eyes over to the backpack Vanessa was holding. "Is that the money?"

"It is," Alinna answered. "Can we see the stuff before anything is traded?"

Smiling again, Geovani looked over to his driver nodded his head then looked back to Alinna as the driver climbed backing the Benz.

Shifting her eyes over to the driver as he climbed from the Benz with two large leather duffel bags, Alinna continued watching as the driver stepped forward, dropping both bags at her feet.

Bending down, opening the second bag, and seeing the weed, Alinna looked to Geovani letting him know she was opening one of the bricks to check the coke receiving a simple nod of the head.

Pulling a butterfly knife that she always carried between her breasts, Alinna opened the knife and cut open one of the bricks making a finger size hole, and then stuck her pinky nail inside the powder scooping out and sticking her nail into her mouth tasting it.

Once her tongue went numb, Alinna nodded her head then looked up at Geovani saying, "This is good."

"So you are satisfied then?" Geovani asked, smiling again.

Nodding her head, Alinna looked to Vanessa saying, "Give 'em the money."

Doing as she was told Vanessa tossed the backpack at the feet of the driver causing him to look down first but then bend down to pick up the backpack.

Hearing the rapid shot's sounding off as soon as the driver hand-gripped the backpack, Alinna saw both Geovani, Mario, and the driver all look right and left at their men. She wasted no time pulling her .380 around just as Mario's headed exploded and his body slammed backwards against the Benz truck.

Meeting Geovani's eyes after seeing what Vanessa just did to Mario, Alinna let her .380 ring out as the front of Geovani chest exploded from the .380 round.

Looking over to the driver and hearing the rapid shots, Alinna saw the driver's body dance as chunks of his body was ripped off. Dante then jogged up with an AK-47 gripped in both hands.

"Miss me, shorty?" Dante asked, smirking at Alinna and then kicked the backpack over to her saying, "Let's get the fuck outta here."

Snatching up the backpack and one of the duffel bags, Vanessa snatched up the other. Alinna followed behind Vanessa when she saw Dre was also with an AK-47 gripping in his hand's catching the smirk he shot as she ignored all the bodies' running back to the Lexus IS 350.

$ $ $

Making it back to Miami in one piece, both Alinna and Vanessa talked the whole drive home. Both were hyper and they expected themselves to be about the whole move they made with Dante and Dre against Geovani. Vanessa pulled the Lexus in front of Alinna townhouse by 1:00 p.m.

"Where the hell are Andre and Dante now?" Vanessa said, realizing the rental Ford Explorer wasn't with them as she and Alinna climbed from the Lexus.

"Girl, I don't know," Alinna answered, smiling and taking the duffel bags from the backseat of the car. She added, "I saw the Explorer when we were on I-95, but I'm starting to get used to them just disappearing like that. Come on let's get this stuff inside the house."

Sucking her teeth as she grabbed the Burberry backpack and both hers and Alinna bag's, Vanessa closed the door and then followed behind Alinna to the front door.

"When are you going to tell Dante about Tony T getting shot?" Vanessa asked as she followed Alinna inside the townhouse.

"Whenever I can actually talk to his ass," Alinna answered as she headed to the den.

Dropping both duffel bags onto the coffee table then dropping down onto the sofa as Vanessa walked into the den with two bottles of Corona Alinna thanked her girl and reached for the duffel bag when her cell phone began ringing.

Sighing at hearing her phone ring, Alinna sat back in the sofa then grabbed her Gucci purse, pulled out her iPhone, and smiled when she realized it was Dante calling.

"You wanna tell me where the hell you at, Dante?"

"Missing me huh?"

Smiling but forcing her voice to sound upset, Alinna said, "You need to answer my questions, Dante."

"You smiling ain't you?"

"Dante!" she yelled, smiling harder.

Laughing, Dante finally answered her, "I'm headed to the crib real quick to change clothes and pick up some stuff. Dre and I already dropped off the rental but I gotta handle some something."

"When am I seeing you?"

"So you do miss me huh?"

"Dante shut up," she told him smiling. "Can you answer the question please?"

"As soon as you admit that you miss me."

Sucking her teeth unable to wipe the smile off her lips Alinna finally admitted, "Alright boy. Damn, yes I miss your ass, now when am I seeing you?"

"I'm gonna hit you up in a little while, but Dre's coming through to make sure you and Vanessa are good."

"So basically you mean he's coming to see Vanessa but you need to hurry up and get here. I got something important I need to talk to you about."

"Talk."

"Not over the phone."

"Are you alright?"

Smiling at his concern for her Alinna answered, "I'm fine Dante. What I must tell you isn't about me. We'll talk when you get here."

"Alright, shorty. I'ma be there in a little while."

"Bye boy," Alinna said hanging up smiling.

"Girl, that boy has got ya ass wide the hell open," Vanessa told Alinna while smiling, as she sat watching her girl the whole time she was on the phone.

"Shut up, Vanessa," Alinna told her rolling her eye's smiling also.

$ $ $

Dante pulled through the front gate of his apartment complex a few minutes after hanging up with Alinna and drove towards the back of the complex to his building. Parking his Altima, he grabbed his backpack from the backseat, when all in one motion after hearing the loud and hard bang on his driver's window, grabbed his burner in his left hand while swinging around towards the driver's door only to catch Angela who stood out in front of his car door with her hand up on her hips and face balled up in anger.

"Open the fucking door, Dante!" Angela yelled from outside the car.

Shaking his head, Dante grabbed his bag and opened the car door.

"Where the fuck have you been and why haven't you been answering my phone calls, Dante?"

Ignoring Angela, Dante walked away from the Altima and headed toward his building opening, while hearing Angela behind him calling his name louder and louder while following closely behind him.

Once he reached his apartment door, he saw the way Angela stood staring at him from the corner of his eye on his right side. Dante unlocked the front door opening it only for Angela to push past him busting into the apartment.

Tempted to pull his burner and open up the back of her dome, Dante shook the thought as he stepped into the apartment, ignoring the staring that he was getting from Angela. He turned and closed the door locking it behind him.

Turning back and facing Angela, Dante went to step past her only to see the slap leaning back out of the range and watching her hands fly pass.

Reaching out to grab her throat before Angela realized what he was doing, Dante tightened his grip around her throat causing her to reach up and grab at his hand.

"Don't ever try me like that again."

Grasping for air once Dante released her throat, Angela grabbed for her sidearm at her hip but froze after hearing Dante's warning, "You pull that shit then you better use it."

Watching him as he walked calmly back to his room at the back of the apartment, Angela angrily followed behind him and stomped into the bedroom yelling, "Dante, you need to fucking tell me where the hell you've been! I've been calling you for three days and you haven't answered none of my phone calls!"

"I've been handling business," Dante answered as he pulled off his shirt and walked over to his closet.

"What business, Dante?" Angela asked, walking up on him. "Why haven't you answered my calls?"

"What do you want Angela?" Dante asked walking by and ignoring her question. "I got stuff to handle."

"I want time with you."

"Later."

"No, now."

"Later," Dante told her repeating himself as he pulled down a fatigue colored Akademic cotton hoody sweat suit while walking over to the bed.

Walking up behind Dante following him over to the bed, Angela reached her arm around him and gripped his manhood in her right hand caressing him. "Dante, I miss you Papi. You haven't answered any of my calls and I've been calling you since Tuesday night. I even called when I heard that your friend Tony T was shot and put in the …"

"What the fuck you said?" Dante snapped, snatching away from Angela staring at her as if she was crazy. "What the fuck you said, bitch?"

"Dante, relax he's doing …"

"Bitch, what happened?" Dante cut her off, staring hard at Angela.

Seeing the look on Dante's face, Angela shook her head as she told Dante about the shootout with Tony T and the unknown shooter.

Hearing all he needed to hear, Dante began undressing and then dressing into the sweat suit that he had laid across the bed.

9

Swinging the Kawasaki Ninja inside parkway hospital where Angela said Tony T were twenty minutes after leaving his apartment complex, Dante found a parking space, parked the bike, and headed across the parking lot hearing his cell phone ringing from inside his pocket. Dante ignored it for a moment because he was pretty sure it was Angela calling him.

Once inside the hospital, Dante asked the nurse at the front desk what room Tony T was in since Angela wouldn't tell him. Dante had to show ID then he was allowed to visit his boy, discovering he was on the third floor in room 310. Taking the elevator up to the third floor, Dante stopped off on the third floor, ignoring the two nurses who were at the call desks staring at him. Looking around and trying to locate 310, he found the room at the very end of the hall. Dante didn't even bother knocking as he pushed the door open to room 310. "Dante," both Kerry and Harmony said in unison upon seeing him.

Hugging Tony T's baby sister, Kerry after she rushed to him, Dante walked over to Tony T's bedside with Kerry hugged onto his side. He nodded to Harmony, and then looked to his boy who laid smiling a small smirk toward him. "How you feeling my nigga?" Dante asked.

"I feel how I look," Tony T replied. "Fuck you been at?"

"Handling business out of town," Dante answered. "What happened? Who did this to you?"

Looking to Harmony then Kerry, Tony T said, "Let me holla at Dante real quick."

Shaking her head and rolling her eyes at Tony T, Harmony called to Kerry, "Let's get something to eat."

Watching both Kerry and Harmony leave the room, Dante looked back to Tony T asking, "How long have you two been kicking it?"

"Since two days after the shit with Big Worm went down," Tony T admitted, but then became serious. "I ain't sure who these dudes were but I got word that all this shit was because of this bitch named Rachel."

"Who the fuck is Rachel?"

"What I hear is this bitch out in the streets bragging about having her brother get at me for playing her like a hoe."

"Okay, so who's her brother?"

"Some chump named, Big Daddy."

"Big *what?*" Dante replied with a look of disbelief on his face. "You got to be kidding me ..."

"Nah, that's what I hear he goes by," Tony T replied. "Homeboy supposed to be the same major coke and heroin pusher out of Alabama."

"That's good news to hear," Dante said smiling. "How long you gotta be in this shit?"

"Doctor's trying to hold me until next week, but I'm leaving this place by Friday. Fuck a doctor."

"You've grown. I'm going to look into this shit with this Big Daddy dude," Dante told Tony T, and then added, "Don't trip about this bitch Rachel, I'm gonna get that handled."

"Bet my nigga," Tony T told his homeboy and dappin him up.

$ $ $

Making it back to her townhouse after making a few sales and dropping off work with Amber, Alinna called Harmony and discovered that she was at the hospital with Tony T after she found that Harmony was not at her apartment. Harmony told Alinna that Dante was also there with Tony T. Alinna walked inside her home as Vanessa drove away to go meet up with Dre at his place. Locking the front door then walking upstairs to her bedroom, Alinna changed into gray cotton sweat pants and an oversized white tee shirt that fell past her hips. She grabbed the backpack she had for Dante and then headed back downstairs, dropping the backpack in the den and headed into the kitchen. Looking through the refrigerator for something to fix for her and Dante to eat, she caught herself smiling at the thought of Dante. Alinna decided to cook chicken wings, yellow rice sweat peas, and butter rolls.

Alinna was halfway finished with the food when she heard Dante's motorcycle pulling up out front. She smiled as she moved the frying pan from the heat then found herself rushing for the door a small smile showing.

"What's up, shorty?" Dante asked, bending to kiss Alinna's lips. She hated how she responded so hungrily for him. Alinna rounded her eyes as she turned back facing the inside of the house. "Where've you been?"

"It smells good up in here," Dante said, ignoring her question. He closed and locked the door behind him. "What you cooking us?"

"I'm cooking *me* something to eat," she said, looking back at him from over her shoulder.

"Oh, something for you, huh?" Dante repeated with a sarcastic tone as he walked into the kitchen stopping behind

Alinna and looking over her shoulder. He smirked seeing the amount of food she had cooked.

"Move Dante," Alinna told him playfully shooing him away from the food.

"You better be really hungry with all that food you made for just your little ass," Dante told her, laughing as he walked over to the fridge.

Still smiling while looking back at Dante as he made himself at home after going through her refrigerator, Alinna shook her head as she focused back on the food. "How is Tony T doing?"

"If you knew where I was, why did you ask?" Dante asked Alinna as he leaned up against the counter with a bottle of Corona in his right hand. "He is doing well though; he's tryin to get out of there by Friday."

"He tell you what happened to him?"

"Yeah, we'll take care of that in a moment."

"Who'd he say shot him?" Alinna asked.

"Some dude," Dante answered taking a drink from the bottle then saying, "He said it's some chick named Rachel who set the whole thing up. From what Tony T says, it's supposed to be some clown out Alabama called, Big Daddy."

"Big *who?*" Alinna looked back from cooking, stopping what she was doing to clarify.

Smiling at Alinna's response, Dante said, "That's the name Tony T said dude goes by. But come to find out that homeboy is supposed to be big time in Alabama." Alinna could hear the change of tone in Dante's voice. The tone and his body language let Alinna know he was plotting something.

She looked back to him and asked, "What's up Dante? What are you plotting now?"

Quiet for a moment and following behind Alinna from the kitchen after taking his plate she had handed him, Dante walked into the den and sat down on the sofa, while Alinna went back into the kitchen, he turned on the 38' flat screen.

"So, what's up?" Alinna asked as she walked back into the den carrying two bottles of Coronas and sitting down beside him. Breaking down what had been on his mind since Tony T had told him about Big Daddy, Dante explained to Alinna how at first he just wanted to make that trip to Alabama and see exactly who this dude was and how he wanted to watch Big Daddy to find out how he operates and runs his shit down in Alabama.

"Dante, I don't know nothing about no heroin," Alinna told him once he finished. "You must know somebody with that mess because I don't."

"We will deal with that once we have to," Dante told her with a mouth full of food. "How long is that stuff from Giovanni gonna last until you gotta re-up?"

"With the work we already we already got and the shit from him it should be at least a month and a half before we will need to get more. That's just until shit really starts to pick up once people find out we really pushing heavier weight," Alinna explained.

"Perfect, that sho99\uld be enough time for me and Dre to handle shit down in Alabama. But first I'ma need you to handle something for me," Dante told Alinna, looking into her eyes.

$ $ $

Lying in bed next to a sleeping Alinna after twenty minutes of a mixture between fucking and lovemaking, Dante thought about his plans concerning Alabama and Big Daddy.

Hearing his phone ringing on the bedside table woke him up; he grabbed the phone and looked upon Alinna curled up beside him. She instinctively curled in closer under him, wrapping her arm around his mid-section.

"What's up, braw?" he answered the call, responding to Dre as his name appeared on the screen.

"I'm outside."

"I'll be down in a second," Dante responded and hung up.

Crawling from under Alinna, Dante climbed out of the bed, and put his boxers and sweat pants on. Then he grabbed the backpack Alinna had left for him in the den. He was walking toward the bedroom door when he heard Alinna's voice. "You better be back in ten minutes and tell Dre I said hi." He smiled as he turned back towards the door after listening in to Alinna's request.

Walking to the front door, Dante unlocked the door and saw Dre leaning on the wall by the door, smoking a Newport cigarette. "What up Bruh?"

"What's good fam?" Dre said, tossing the Newport and then stepping inside the house. Locking the front door behind Dre, Dante tossed the backpack onto the coffee table. "I need you to put that up for me. It's a little over $10,000."

"Oh shit, you trying to finally save some money now?" Dre asked jokingly as he sat on the left of Dante on the sofa.

"It's for Alinna," Dante told his boy in all seriousness as he cleared his throat and started over. "If something jumps off, I want her to be straight." Surprised at the way Dante was talking, Dre listened and felt for Dante. He had never heard him talk the way he was at this exact moment.

Dre changed the subject. "So what's up? What you wanted to holla at me about?"

"You went and seen Tony T yet?" Dante asked.

"Yeah I went earlier; he told me you had already came by."

"So you know what's up right? You know what happened to him?"

"Yeah he told me what's up. So what we planning on fam, because I already know you been planning on something?"

"We are gonna take a trip out Alabama, pay this Big Daddy clown a visit."

"We're not just going to visit," Dante finished saying, looking at Dre with a smile on his lips. He began to go into detail on what he had been plotting on and how things would be handled.

10

Leaving the mall after a night of shopping, Rachel was on her way to Club Light with her girls Stacey and Brittany. She headed out to her Cadillac CTS inside of the parking lot at Saw Grass Mills mall. Hearing her cell phone ring from inside her Coach bag as she walked up on the diver side of her car, Rachel unlocked her car, opened the door, and tossed her bag onto the backseat after retrieving her phone. Her phone read 'Stacey' across it. "Hey girl what's up?" Stacey listened to her talk about some new guy she had wanted to introduce her to since she wasn't messing with Tony T's sorry lying ass anymore. Rachel smiled thinking about Tony in the hospital for doing her that way.

Cranking up her car, Rachel put the C.T.S. in reverse. She was just backing out of her parking spot when she slammed on her brakes. A car had suddenly appeared behind her. Hearing and feeling the slight bump she ended up still experiencing, she yelled, "Shit!"

Seeing the Spanish girl as she climbed out of the Lexus and noticing the Gucci outfit she had on and willing to admit the girl was pretty, Rachel got out of the car and walked around to access the damage that had been done. "I'm sorry," the Spanish women told Rachel. "I was on the phone with my boyfriend and I wasn't paying attention."

"It's alright," Rachel told the girl not noticing anything wrong with her car. She smiled at the Spanish girl. "I wasn't really paying attention myself. I was on the phone with my friend, talking about some guy."

"I know how that goes," replied the Spanish girl. "You look familiar; you talk to Tony T right?"

"Girl, not no more," Rachel said rolling her eyes. "I had to get rid of him. Fuck that lying ass nigga."

"I heard he's in the hospital."

"That is good for his ass."

"Why you say that girl? Tony T is good people ..."

"Girl, his ass ain't shit, and between you and me, I had my brother put his ass where he's at. He's lucky I didn't tell my brother to kill him for all the shit he put me through."

"Well I know how it can be with dudes," she told Rachel. "I'm sorry girl. Hey, I'm Alinna."

"Rachel. I have heard your name before," she told her. "Don't you sell weed or something?"

"I use to sell just weed, but since I started messing with my boo, it changed a little. You probably even know my man ..."

"What's his name?" Rachel asked.

"Ask him, he's right there."

"What?" Rachel turned around, and when she did, she felt a fist hit her in the face. Catching Rachel just as she was falling backwards, Dante scooped her up and put her in the passenger side of the C.T.S. Dante sat her in and strapped her seatbelt.

Turning around to Alinna who was holding the door for him, he said, "I'm gonna call you in twenty minutes. Once I am finished, you go ahead and handle your business."

"I will see you later," Alinna told Dante, kissing him then walking over to her car.

Watching Alinna drive off, Dante waited until she disappeared then walked to the driver's side and got into Rachel's car. Seeing the keys were still in the ignition, Dante started the car and reached for his phone. Backing out of the parking spot, he dialed Dre.

"Yeah what up fam?" Dre answered.

"Meet me at Alinna old spot, that apartment. I picked up shorty."

"I'm on my way."

Dante hung up the phone and looked over to the still knocked out Rachel. He smiled. Time for the next part of his plans.

11

Two days after **Dante, Dre, and Tony T left for** Alabama, Alinna got in contact with Narcotics Sergeant Miguel Ruiz. After spending nearly an hour on the phone talking to him, she calmed him down enough to agree to meet up with her them to sit down and talk alone. She also wanted to paint a picture that would make him believe that he would be getting some pussy once they met up.

On the night they agreed to meet, Alinna dressed in a tight body-hugging Gucci outfit that showed her every curve with a pair of stiletto heels.

Leaving her townhouse at 8:00 p.m., Alinna drove her Lexus IS350 while calling Miguel phone.

"Alinna?" Miguel answered on the first ring.

"Were you expecting someone else, Miguel?"

"Where are you?"

"That's why I'm calling. What restaurant are we meeting at?"

"Change of plans," Miguel told her. "We're meeting at the Best Western on 62nd Street and 14th Avenue."

"That's a hotel, Miguel. What are…"

"Alinna look, you owe me for that bullshit in… You know what I want. You've been playing with me for too long and now you have a choice. Give me what I want or I'm turning you in."

"What about Dante?"

"Fuck him," Miguel spit into the phone. "You don't have to tell that piece of shit anything."

After a moment of silence, Alinna finally spoke, "If I do this, are we even?"

"Are you agreeing or what?"

"Miguel, I need to know if this will be over if I do this with you?"

"Alright yeah, give me what I want and I'll forget all of the shit. Now are you coming or what?"

"I'm coming Miguel."

"You will real soon, a whole fucking lot," Miguel replied as he hung up the phone.

Hearing Miguel end the call, Alinna called Vanessa's phone.

"Yeah," Vanessa answered at the start of the first ring.

"Change of plans," Alinna told her, going into a new plan that she came up with while talking to Miguel over the phone.

$ $ $

Pulling inside the Best Western where she was supposed to meet Miguel, Alinna found a parking spot, parked the Lexus, grabbed her Gucci bag, and climbed from the car while locking it. As she walked from the Lexus, Alinna looked around the parking lot and spotted Miguel's Chevy Malibu.

Once inside the hotel lobby, Alinna checked with the front desk only to receive a room key with Miguel's room number on it.

"Room 107," Alinna repeated to the desk clerk.

"Yes ma'am," the clerk told Alinna. Smiling at her thanking the women, Alinna walked off then headed toward the back area where all the hotel room was, finally finding the room after a few minutes of searching.

Using her key, she unlocked the hotel room door, opened the door, stepped inside the room, and closed the door back behind her as she called out to Miguel.

Walking further into the darkened room and seeing the shine from a single lamp, she quickly saw the light on the bedside table on and also saw Miguel laid across the bedside wearing nothing but a pair of black boxers and smiling at her.

"I was wondering what was taking you so long," Miguel told Alinna, as he looked her body over. "Take that shit off and get in bed."

"Slow down," Alinna told him with a smile. "Let me go freshen up and then I'm all yours for the night."

Turning and heading to the bathroom and looking back over her shoulder at Miguel, she saw him watching her caressing his already hardened print through his boxers.

Feeling his heart continue to beat faster, hyped the hell up, Miguel couldn't believe he was actually about to get Alinna to give up the pussy after chasing her from behind for way to long.

Wondering what was taking her so long after five minutes in the bathroom Miguel was just about to call out to her when he heard the bathroom door open then close only to see Alinna walk back out into the bed area fully dressed. "What the hell? Why aren't you naked?"

"I've changed my mind," Alinna told Miguel, watching his facial expression change. "Relax though, I bought something for you."

"What the hell are you..." seeing Alinna along with Amber and Harmony, he quickly noticed the weapon in all three of their hands. Miguel made a dive for his sidepiece over the bedside night table just as heard the blast start from one of the three guns. He felt the bullets slam into his back just a second before the room was lit up the sounds of the three different gun's ringing out inside the room.

Watching Miguel's body jump and jerk all over the bed as bullets slammed into him, Alinna tapped first and then Amber. Harmony got their attention and said, "Let's get out of here."

$ $ $

Hearing about the murder of both the hotel worker, Amber Hill and Narcotics Sergeant Miguel Ruiz, Dante sat listening to the broadcast news about a cop killing in Miami all the way in Alabama. Recognizing the cops name instantly but keeping it to himself, he decided not to mention it to Dre or Tony T.

Deciding against calling home to Alinna and finding out what the deal was with Miguel, Dante focused back on getting ready for the night's mission.

Finishing dressing in the metallic black jeans, white and black Prada short sleeve shirt, all white air max and a leather jacket, Dante grabbed his two .40's and tucked one in front of his jeans and the other in his back. He was startled at the sound of knocking at his motel room door.

Grabbing his room key and then walking over to his room door, Dante opened the door and saw Dre and Tony T dressed and waiting for him outside his room door.

"Fam, you seen the news?" Dre asked Dante as he was locking the room door.

"Yeah," Dante answered taking the joint that Tony T held out to him. "I just saw that shit just now."

"Whoever did the boy gave it to his ass," Tony T said as they headed out to the parking lot. "Dude took more than fifty-something bullets, that's some real live mafia shit right there."

"Fuck that cracker," Dante said, stepping in the passenger door to the rented navigator.

Dante sat in the front seat next to Dre with Tony T in the back.

Dante pulled out his blacks while asking Dre if he had the package they were supposed to have sent to Big Daddy.

Patting his right pocket Dre said, "Everything ready fam," nodding his head as he blew the cigar smoke towards the ceiling of the truck. Dante allowed his mind to focus on his plan's preparing himself.

$ $ $

It was nearly midnight by the time Dre pulled on the strip that the nightclub was on. Dante had Dre let Tony T out in front of the club, telling him to pay their way inside.

Dre found a place to park a block from the club. Both Dante and Dre headed up the street towards the club, ignoring the calls from the girls they passed.

Ignoring the large crowd as they walked to the front door of the club, Dante allowed Dre to step forward in front of him, making an opening through the crowd. Hearing and ignoring the people complaining, Dre pushed out of the way.

Hearing the loud whistle and seeing Tony T standing at the front door of Club Ebony, Dante felt a hand grab his arm just as he was getting ready to step up to the front door. Looking down at his arm, he recognized the woman's hand as he looked up to meet the owner hands.

"Damn, daddy, you just gonna walk right past me and not say anything?" the female said, looking Dante over loving what she was seeing.

Smirking, Dante simply nodded his head, saying, "Come on, shorty. You're with me."

"What about my girls?" she asked him while pointing back to her girls.

Looking from the cute-but-thick, dark brown-skinned shorty to the two girls that she was with, Dante nodded and looked back to shorty with the banging body. "Bring ya girls, come on."

Seeing the smile upon all three girls face, Dante allowed Ms. Thick to hold onto his arm as he headed straight up to the front door, receiving nods from both security at the front door.

Once inside the night club that was even more crowded then it was outside, Dante led the group over to the bar while searching the club for Big Daddy. He looked for the same picture of the fat motherfucker that was inside of Rachel's cell phone.

"You and ya girls want something to drink?" Dante asked Ms. Thick, who eagerly bobbed her head up and down.

Having Tony T order each of the girls what they wanted, Dante continued looking around for Big Daddy when he felt the tap on his shoulder. He looked to Dre on his right only to see his boy nod upwards.

Looking in the direction Dre nodded, Dante found himself staring straight through the glass window into the V.I.P. section up on the second level, and saw the fat motherfucker he was looking for.

Nodding his head as he continued watching Big Daddy, Dante shifted his eye's over to Ms. Thick as she walked up on him smiling.

"You good, shorty?"

"I'm doing fine so far," she answered, and then asked, "Where you and your boy's from? You don't sound like you from here."

Ignoring her question, Dante asked, "You and your girls wanna make two hundred a piece?"

"Damn, you don't waste no time do you sexy?" she asked Dante, smiling at him. "What it's gonna be? Us and you, or all six of us?"

Shaking his head smirking, Dante said, "You misunderstanding me, shorty, I just need you and your girl to deliver something to someone for me."

"Deliver what?" she asked him, staring at Dante with a funny look on her face. Calling over to Dre, telling him to give him the envelope, Dante took the envelope from him and handed it over to Ms. Thick.

"Where's the money?" she asked, holding out her left hand while hiding the envelope in her right hand.

"I'll throw in an extra hundred if you keep what's inside this closed and inside," Dante told her, pulling a knot from his pocket, counting out seven hundred dollars in all hundreds, and handing the money over to the girl.

Watching Ms. Thick and her girls walk off together, Dante followed Ms. Thick with his eyes, hearing Dre ask, "You think she'll be able to get past the security at the stairs?"

Still watching as all three girls stopped at the steps that led up into the V.I.P. section, seeing words being exchanged a few moments, Dante allowed a small smile at seeing Ms. Thick kiss both security men on their cheeks then led her girls up the steps into V.I.P.

$ $ $

Finding out who was up inside the V.I.P. section from the security downstairs, recognizing Big Daddy's name, and meeting him once before when he came through the strip club she worked at, Brittany lead her girls inside of the packed V.I.P. section, smiling. The room was filled with weed smoke with over ten different opened bottles and even more on top of the table.

Barely making it fully inside the V.I.P. section before her and her girl was rushed by a group of niggas grabbing and feeling all over them, Brittany took a minute to make her way over to where Big Daddy was seated with a thick white girl on his lap, and his hand under her skirt as she rubbed between his legs.

"What's up, baby?" Brittany heard as she stopped in front of Big Daddy's table. She recognized the dark skinned guy that was slightly smaller than the big dude that was with Mr. Sexy who got her and her girls inside the club.

"I got something for Big Daddy," Brittany told the guy, seeing the big ass gun on his waist.

"Let me get it," he told her. "I'll get it to Big Daddy."

She said, "Fuck it," after only agreeing to get the envelope to Big Daddy. Brittany gave the letter to the guy, turned, and walked off.

Watching the thick as hell female walk away, Dave shook his head as he looked down at the envelope and opening it, seeing it was full of pictures.

Pulling out the seven pictures, Dave looked at the first two, seeing a beat up and bloodied female. As he looked at the third one, he almost dropped the pictures recognizing Big Daddy's baby sister, Rachel.

"Shit," Dave said as he finished looking through the pictures only to see a letter with only a phone number two words on it. 'Call me,' it read.

Walking over to Big Daddy, Dave got his boss attention saying, "You may wanna see this."

$ $ $

Watching from the front passenger's seat outside the club within the rental car, a crowd of guys burst out the front doors of the club noticing Ms. Thick and her girls forcefully being dragged out of the club. Dante locked on Big Daddy, angrily walking with a wall of bodyguards from the club's front door and out to the black Benz truck that pulled up in front of the club.

Continuing to watch until the Benz drove out of the parking lot along with two black Escalades trailing behind, Dante finally spoke, saying over to Dre, "Let's go braw."

Doing as he was told, Dante cranked up the rental and pulled off, only to make a U-turn, driving in the opposite direction from Big Daddy and his crew.

"What's up, Dee? What we doing now?" Tony T asked from the back seat.

"Wait," Dante told Tony T only to hear the pre-paid cell phone he bought ringing from inside his pocket moments after he finish speaking.

Knowing exactly who was calling since only one person had the pre-paid cell number, Dante pulled out the phone and answered it, "Yeah."

"Motherfucker what the…"

He hung up in Big Daddy's face in the middle his sentence, not liking the tone of his voice. Dante started to countdown the time in his head and reached a count of four when the phone started to ring again. "We trying this again, yeah?"

"Man who the hell are you?" Big Daddy asked in an upset but calmer voice. "Where's my sister?"

"Listen, because I'm only saying this once, you got until tomorrow night at exactly 11:00 p.m. to have $250,000 and two bricks of that heroin you pushing. Have the shit at the Pine Hill mall on the south side parking lot. You got that?"

"Where's my sister?"

You'll see her when I get what I want," Dante told Big Daddy, hanging up the phone just as Big Daddy was yelling something back through the phone.

$ $ $

Going about business as if nothing happened after the setup on Miguel the night before, Alinna heard talk of the cop killing with the added body of the hotel worker. Everybody was trying to figure out how the two were connected hearing that the women was married and talk of her and Miguel hooking up behind the husband's back.

Dealing with a new problem made her want Dante home even more now. Not hearing from him but once since Dre, Tony T, and him left for Alabama, Alinna was confused at first with the way she was feeling, only to set an appointment and find out that she was nearly a month pregnant.

Telling Vanessa about the pregnancy expecting her to actually start tripping out about the whole thing, she was surprised to first see the huge smile and hadn't expected her to hug her inside of a huge bear hug.

"I'm gonna be an auntie," Vanessa cried excitedly still hugging Alinna.

Pulling away from Vanessa smiling at her girl, Alinna fixed her clothes and said, "I'm happy that you're happy, but I'm worried about what Dante's going to say."

"What can he say?" Vanessa said and then added, "He's gonna be a daddy, he'll be happy, Alinna."

"I'm hoping he is happy, but we never talked about a baby or us having one. Then look at the shit we're into, I just hope he ready for a baby, Vanessa," Alinna told her girl, explaining as her smiled slipped a little at a time until it was completely gone.

12

Parked inside the Pine Hills mall parking lot, positioned in the opening where they could easily be seen at from the front entrance of the mall entrance, Dante first saw the Escalade, and then another Escalade pulling inside the mall parking lot, until finally seeing the Benz truck as it pulled inside the parking lot behind the two Escalades.

Looking down at his Mickey Mouse watch and seeing Big Daddy was three minutes late, Dante looked back up in time to see all three SUV's pulling up in front of the rental, keeping a few feet back from them.

"Come on," Dante told Dre, climbing out of the rental, and walking around the front end of the rental. Dante positioned himself up against the front end of the truck, watching as Big Daddy exited the Benz truck and walked through the crowd of twelve bodyguards who were all gripping burners in their hands.

"Where the fuck is my sister?" Big Daddy asked, as he started stared at both men he had ever seen before.

Ignoring Big Daddy's question, Dante calmly asked, "Where's the stuff I said I wanted?"

"Where the fuck is my sister you bitch ass motherfucker?" Big Daddy said repeating himself.

"I'm starting to get upset," Dante said, still leaning against the front of the rental truck. "Last time asking and then you won't have to worry about where your sister's at. She'll be with wherever it is a bitch goes after I put a bullet in their head. Where's my money and heroin, fat boy?"

Starting at the motherfucker who spoke to him, promising himself that he would kill the motherfucker before him or the big motherfucker he was with left the parking lot, Big Daddy called out to somebody named Cole. He watched one of the bodyguards that Big Daddy called out, walk off from the group, stop over next to one of the Escalades opening the back door, and pulled out two black briefcases. Dante shifted his eyes back to Big Daddy finding the fat bastard staring straight at him. "Everything better be there."

"Everything's there," Big Daddy replied, motioning for Cole to take the briefcase to the guys.

Watching as the bodyguards stepped forward, Dante tapped the front end of the rental truck, and Dante stepped forward to meet the guy.

Once Dre had both briefcases and was back beside Dante, he laid both briefcases on top of the truck's hood opening them both.

Looking over to his left seeing the briefcase filled with money while the other had two bricks of heroin inside, Dante saw Dre check under a few of the stacks of bills just as Big Daddy called out again, asking where his sister was.

Slowly smiling as Dre closed the briefcase, Dante looked back to Big Daddy saying, "Your sister is close by, but answer one question before I tell you exactly where's she's at."

"What the fuck now?" Big Daddy asked loudly.

"You know someone named Tony T who used to fuck with your sister, Rachel?" Dante asked, still smiling a small smirk.

"Who the fuck you talking about? Who the fuck is Tony T?" Big Daddy yelled starting to lose his patience.

Shaking his head Dante laughed as he looked to his left saying. "Hey yo, Tony T. He don't even remember you braw, crazy shit."

"This is fucked up," Tony T said as he stepped into view after watching from the dark shadows at the side of the corner of the mall's front entrance front doors.

Hearing another voice, he turned his attention to his right just as his men's yelled in warning. Big Daddy had enough time to see the dark brown-skinned guy with the AR-15 gripped in both hands right before the poorly lit parking lot lit up with the AR-15 he was holding.

$ $ $

After dropping Vanessa off at home feeling unwell, but feeling better than she did the previous night, Alinna told her girl to call her later as she walked up to the front door to her town house.

Hearing her cell phone ring as she pulled her keys from her purse, Alinna unlocked her front door, turned back to wave at Vanessa, and then pulled her cell phone from her left side pocket.

Breaking out in a huge smile at seeing Dante calling, Alinna answered as she stepped inside the house. "Hey baby, where are you? You still in Alabama? How long you planning on being there? When are you coming home? I miss you."

"Damn shorty, you plan on breathing?" Dante asked laughing.

Smiling at his response, but smiling harder Alinna asked again, "When are you getting home?"

"We should be in Miami by morning sometime around 3:00."

"So everything went okay there in Alabama?"

"Everything went good, shorty?"

Smiling harder, Alinna said, "Well, I've gotta talk to you when you get home. It's important."

"Talk."

"Not over the…"

"You said it was important, shorty. Talk"

"Dante it can wait until you get home. We're okay and it's all okay, alright?"

"We'll be there in a few hours."

Hearing the anger in his voice recognizing Dante was upset, she simply couldn't tell him what she had to tell him. Alinna also noticed he didn't catch her little clue that she gave him with the whole, "We're okay," thing she said. "I love you Dante."

"Yeah, love you too, Alinna," Dante told her, but hung up the phone right afterwards.

Shaking her head smiling again after Dante hung up the phone Alinna headed up to her bedroom to shower and change into something to where to bed.

$ $ $

Not sure how long she was asleep or when she fell asleep, Alinna opened her eyes, feeling someone brushing the side of her face gently with his hands, slowly smiling once she realized she was seeing Dante seated beside her on the bed. "Hey baby, you just got here?"

"Yeah," Dante answered, brushing back her hair from her face.

"How you feeling?"

"I'm good, I just miss you?" Alinna told him, sitting up and hugging Dante around the neck.

"How's the baby?" Dante asked, speaking into Alinna's ear.

Pulling back and looking at Dante in complete surprise, Alinna stared into Dante's eyes for a moment. "Who told you?"

"You did," Dante answered, and then said, "I caught on to what you said after we hung up the phone. The whole *we're* okay and it's okay comment."

"I was wondering if you would catch that."

"I try not to miss too much."

"Are you mad or happy?"

"Why would I be mad?" Dante asked, staring at Alinna with questioning eyes.

"I just thought that with what we've been doing that you wouldn't be ready for us to have a baby yet," Alinna explained to him.

"Shorty listen," Dante started, kicking off his shoes, and then pulling out both .40's, laying one of the bedside table, and then sliding the other under his pillow only to feel another burner. He pulled it out only to see Alinna's .380.

"You weren't home," Alinna told him, taking her gun, and sticking it under her own pillow as she moved over to her side of the bed.

Laying down beside Alinna as she laid her head on his chest, Dante admitted what he was saying. "I don't worry about you handling business and what not, but I've thought about that too and I'm changing up things a little bit. You can continue doing your thing with Vanessa, Harmony, and Amber, but I'm gonna deal with the problems my way without you. I want you to focus on stacking this case and getting us rich, you good with that?"

"I don't know if I have a choice," Alinna answered rubbing her hand under his shirt, rubbing his stomach feeling his six pack and hard muscles.

"One more thing," Dante told her, causing Alinna to raise her head to meet his eyes. "You got something you wanna tell me?"

"Like what?" Alinna asked with a confused look on her face.

"Miguel?" Dante asked, smirking at Alinna.

Slowly smiling, Alinna laid her head back down onto her man's chest and went into explaining about Miguel finding out about the Geovani hit and then explaining about Miguel's threats to turn them in if she wouldn't sleep with him, which was how she set up the hit at the hotel where both Amber and Harmony killed Miguel.

"Where was Vanessa while you, Amber, and Harmony were handling ole boy.

"You heard about the white girl named Amber who's being called Miguel's mistress?" Alinna asked, looking back up at Dante.

"Yeah, who's she?" Dante asked holding Alinna eyes.

"She wasn't nobody really, just a hotel clerk," Alinna answered. "But she's the reason Vanessa wasn't in the room with us."

"So Vanessa was putting shorty to sleep while y'all deaded that clown, Miguel?" Dante asked, smiling as he shook his head. "You women are really something else."

"We learned from the best," Alinna told Dante, smiling at him. "What you get from the hit in Alabama?"

"It's in the closet," Dante told her, watching as Alinna climbed out of bed and walked over to the closet pulling out the two briefcase and walking back over to the bed.

Laying both briefcases on top of the bed, Alinna opened one and saw the heroin. Dante announce that one briefcase was filled with two bricks of heroin that she broke into while the other was packed with $250,000.

Looking over to Dante in shock and surprise, Alinna opened the other briefcase and saw that it was in fact filled with money. She looked back to Dante asking him, "What happened to Big Daddy and Rachel after you, Dre, and Tony T got the money and drugs?

"You already know what happened with Big Daddy's fat ass, but Rachel never made it out of Miami," Dante told her, winking his eye.

Shaking her head smiling, Alinna said, "I want you to chill for a while."

"Chill? For what?" Dante asked, staring at Alinna with a questionable stare.

"Baby, we have enough work to last us at least until after the baby is born. I'm already one month into this pregnancy and I want us to move in together," Alinna told him, and then added, "I want us all to move in together."

"All of us, as in me, you, the girls and Dre?"

"Tony T also, since he's messing with Harmony."

Quiet for a moment while thinking, Dante finally said, "Alright, I'm with the whole living together idea, but I'm not with the whole laying back doing nothing idea."

Sighing, Alinna smiled and said, "Alright, you Dre, Tony T, can do a few small jobs outside of Florida, but nothing major until after the baby is born, Dante."

Smiling, Dante said, "Now that's an idea I'm with shorty."

"I bet you are," Alinna replied, smiling as she closed both brief cases, winking at Dante.

13

Bringing up the idea to the others about everyone moving in together and getting everyone to agree, Alinna, Vanessa, Amber, and Harmony looked for a new house that everyone was going to move into, only for Dante, Dre, and Tony T to up and leave the state again after hearing about some pill dealer in South Carolina who went by the name, Snoop.

Finding a large enough house for all seven of them, Alinna went ahead and put a down payment on the house, while Dante, Dre, and Tony T were still out of town handling their business.

Once the paperwork was complete, the real estate agent gave them the okay to move in, Alinna and the girls went shopping for the new house and even hiring a new housekeeper and cook for the house. She was an older motherly-type of black woman named, Rosa.

By the time Dante, Dre, and Tony T returned from South Carolina, nearly everything was finished with the new house.

"Damn shorty, you don't miss ya man?" Dante asked, smiling as he walked into the bedroom seeing Alinna packing her stuff.

Leaning back into him as Dante wrapped his arms around her from the back and hugging him back, Alinna raised her lips accepting the kiss Dante gave her, and then nodded over to the backpack that he dropped by the door. "What's in the bag?"

"I miss you too," Dante told her, releasing Alinna only to playfully slap her on the ass before walking over to pick up the Louie Vuitton backpack and toss it over onto the bed as he walked to the foot of the bed.

"What's up? You're moving and didn't tell me about it?" Dante asked, having just noticed the room was empty while pulling out three clear extra-large sandwich bags filled with molly pills.

"If you would have called me, you would have known what was going on while you were gone," Alinna told him as she picked up one of the sandwich bags. "How many pills are these?"

"Five thousand," Dante answered, ignoring the look she shot him. "What do you mean 'what's going on while I was out?'"

Rolling her eyes as she tossed the sandwich bags onto the bed next to the backpack, Alinna went back to packing saying, "We already found a new place. It's a new house that's half furnished and whenever you and your boys finish jumping from state to state, we can move in."

Ignoring her attitude because of her pregnancy, Dante walked up behind her, wrapping his arms around her waist, and laying his hands on her stomach as he spoke into her ear, "Come on shorty, you know I'm there whenever you need me. Alinna all you gotta do is call and anything and everything I'm doing will stop, you know that Alinna."

A quiet moment after listening to Dante, knowing he meant exactly what he said to her, Alinna dropped the clothes she was folding and reached up and back with her right hand, grabbing Dante behind the neck as she learned her head up kissing him in a passionate kiss.

Breaking after a moment, Alinna turned facing Dante saying, "I want to move into our house today."

Nodding his head, Dante pulled out his cell phone and called Dre.

"Yeah fam, what's up?" Dre answered.

"Braw we got to handle something real quick," Dante told his boy while staring at Alinna watching the smile slowly spread across his lips.\

$ $ $

Giving Alinna what she wanted with Dre and Tony T's help, Dante emptied her condo and his apartment out. After thirty minutes of being instructed where to arrange furniture,

Dante, Dre and Tony T finally finished working and felt as if they were free moving men.

After getting a better look around the new two-story, four-bedroom, two-and-a-half-bath, and four-car garage house, Dante allowed Alinna to drag him from the kitchen to meet the new housekeeper named Rose who he instantly liked. They then ended up outside in the large backyard only to see Vanessa, Harmony, and Amber all inside the massive ten-foot swimming pool while both Dre and Tony T stood talking to a dark-skinned, shaved-head guy who was smoking a cigarette.

"Who's homeboy?" Dante asked Alinna while staring straight at the guy.

"Relax baby," Alinna told Dante, smiling as she rubbed his chest, seeing that look he got when seeing new people. "That's Amber's boyfriend."

"What is he doing here?" Dante asked still staring at the guy.

"I'm going to talk to you about that later," Alinna told him just as Amber called out to Dante from the pool.

Shifting his eyes from the guy over to Amber as she climbed from the pool wearing a baby blue two-piece bathing suit, Dante looked back over to the guy seeing him and both Dre and Tony T now staring over to him.

"Dante," Amber said, smiling as she jogged up beside him grabbing his hand. "I want you to meet somebody. Please give him a chance, Dante."

Looking over to the poolside where Harmony and Vanessa sat leaning on the edge of the pool, Alinna locked eyes with Vanessa seeing the questioning look on her girls face.

Shaking her head as she looked from Vanessa while following a step behind Dante and Amber, Alinna stepped beside her man as Amber introduced her boyfriend to Dante.

"Dante, this is my boyfriend Wesley," Amber told Dante but then looked to her man saying, "Wesley, this is who we've been telling you about."

Holding out his hand to Dante, Wesley said, "What's up rude boy? I've been hearing of you, it's good to meet you brethren.

Ignoring Wesley's hand but recognizing Wesley's accent, Dante switched his English to a Jamaican Patois saying, "What part of Jamaica you from?"

Smiling at hearing his own language, surprised at how good Dante spoke Patois, Wesley replied also in Patois, "I'm from Kingston, brethren, you a Rastaman?"

Nodding his head that he was, Dante continued in Patois saying, "My father was a dread, and my mother was American. How you meet Amber?"

Explaining how he and Amber met a few months back while he was making a drop-off with some work he was getting rid of, Amber got into it with some dude and a female. He later found out Ambers dude at the time and the female was the dude's lady on the side. Wesley broke down how he helped out.

"Where's homeboy now?" Dante asked, switching back to English as he held Wesley eyes.

"Let's just say a blood clot don't have no worries now," Wesley told Dante, smiling a small devious smile.

Nodding his head slowly as he held Wesley's dark brown eyes, Dante broke eye contact looking over to Amber saying, "Why didn't you tell me you had a problem with some clown you was messing with?"

Looking to Wesley but looking back to Dante seeing the way he was staring at her, Amber cut her eyes over to Alinna, and then looked back at Dante again saying, "I never got a chance to say anything. Wesley handled it before I could say anything. You mad?"

Shaking his head that he wasn't, Dante said, "Just tell us what's going and whether it's handled or not. Don't leave us in the blind. But I'm pretty sure Alinna, Vanessa and Harmony knew about this."

Watching Dante turn and walk off with Alinna following behind him, Amber looked to Dre asking, "Dre, he mad ain't he?"

"Naw," Dre answered shaking his head. "If fam was mad, you'd be looking for a new boyfriend cause ole boy Wesley here would already be taking that trip to see the good lord."

$ $ $

"Where'd you learned to speak Patois?" Alinna asked Dante as she stood at the breakfast bar while Rose handed him a bottle of Corona from the refrigerator.

"My pop's," Dante answered nodding his thanks to Rose, but then looked to Alinna meeting her stare. "My pop's was Jamaican. I learned it before he was killed."

"No wonder you are like you are. You a dread and all y'all are crazy," Alinna said jokingly but then turned serious asking, "So what do you think about Wesley?"

"Why?" Dante asked, lowering the bottle from his lips shifting his eyes to Alinna.

Sighing softly, Alinna admitted, "Amber and Vanessa came to me about putting Wesley up with us."

"Us what?" Dante asked sitting his bottle down and staring hard at Alinna.

Looking to Rose and seeing the older women walk out the kitchen, Dante turned to Alinna who said, "Wesley sells weed and he just lost his connect because of something that happened, but he also knows a few spots you, Dre, and Tony

T can hit. But I've already made my decision. I'm just letting you know my decision."

"Well handle ya business since you already made your decision," Dante told her as he turned away, leaving the kitchen just as his cell phone went off.

Watching Dante walk off, Alinna shook her head as she heard the double doors leading to the backyard opening looking back seeing Amber, Harmony, and Vanessa walking inside the house.

"What happened, A?" Amber asked as she, Vanessa and Harmony stopped beside Alinna.

"Y'all know how Dante is, he don't trust nobody," Alinna told her girls. "He gotta get to know Wesley before he get cool enough to have him around."

"So you told him about Wesley working with us on opening up a trap house?" Vanessa asked.

"I never got a chance before he got mad and walked off," Alinna said just as Dante walked back up with his faced balled up and pissed off.

"Hit me up on my cell phone if you need me, I gotta handle something," Dante told Alinna, and then looked to Vanessa saying, "Nessa, walk with me. I wanna holla at you right quick."

"Where are you about to go, Dante?" Alinna asked him as he Vanessa was walking off.

"Call me if you need me," Dante told Alinna, repeating himself and then turning away continuing towards the front of the house.

Cursing in Spanish under her breath, Alinna sat watching both Dante and Vanessa walk away from her.

Once outside and over at the garage door at the far right side of the house, Dante got the garage door opened, but turned back to Vanessa ignoring how good she looked in her two-piece bathing suit that she was wearing, realizing why his boy Dre was going crazy for the girl. He said, "Vanessa look, Alinna told me about this shit with Amber dude locking in with us. I don't know homeboy, but I'm holding you responsible for this dude because I know Alinna is doing this more for you instead of Amber. So if this dude gets wrong, I expect you to deal with homeboy or I'm gonna deal with him and then I'm gonna deal with everybody that's connected with him no matter who the person is or if I got love for the person. Now are we clear?"

Understanding Dante clearly, as she stood staring into his eyes, Vanessa nodded her head saying, "I got you Dante. Don't worry."

"Good looking out," Dante told her as he walked in the garage where his bike was.

Once on his Kawasaki Ninja, Dante backed his bike out, stopping next to Vanessa as she stood still watching him. "I actually do like you a lot, Nessa. Don't let me down shorty."

Slowly smiling, Vanessa said, "Relax, I got you," Winking his eyes allowed a small smile, which caused Vanessa to smile even harder.

Dante cranked up the bike but yelled, "Now get back inside before Dre comes out here and cut up about you dressed like that."

Laughing as she stood watching Dante ride off, Vanessa shook her head unable to help, admitting she actually cared about and liked him as well.

14

Pulling inside the shopping center parking lot twenty minutes after leaving for an open parking space, he found an open spot where a Dodge Caravan was pulling out. Parking the bike and shutting off the engine, Dante swung his head around at hearing the car horn behind him.

Pulling off his helmet, Dante climbed off the bike and walked over to the driver's window. "What do you want, Angela?"

"Get in the car, Dante," Angela ordered, rolling the window up in his face.

Cursing to himself as he walked around the car, Dante climbed inside the Malibu only for Angela to pull off before he could fully close the car door.

Repeating himself again, Dante asked, "What do you want now, Angela?"

"Who the fuck is Alinna, Dante?"

"What?" Dante asked in surprise, looking over to Angela.

"You heard what the fuck I said. Who is she to you?"

"What you talking about?"

"Nigga, don't fucking play with me," Angela yelled looking over to Dante. "Are you fucking this bitch?"

"Who told you about Alinna?" Dante asked, controlling his anger as he stared at Angela.

"I have my ways to keep up with you, that's how I know you have been helping this bitch out. Now answer my fucking question, Dante. Are you fucking her?"

"What does that have to do with you?"

"What?" she screamed, swinging her head back around to Dante. "Motherfucker it has everything to do with me when my child's father is fucking some other bitch."

Staring at Angela in disbelief, not sure that he heard her right, Dante asked, "What the fuck you just said?"

"You heard me nigga, I'm fucking pregna..."

"Bitch say it," Dante spit out, Glock already in his right hand and pressed to the side of Angela head.

"What are you gonna do, kill me?" Angela asked feeling her heart beating harder than she ever felt it beat before. "I'm carrying your fucking child and you wanna kill me? Are you forgetting that I'm also a police sergeant?"

Cursing as he snatched his burner away from against Angela's head, Dante cursed even louder and slammed his fist into the dashboard causing Angela to jump in fear and surprise. "Tell me this is bullshit, Angela?"

"I'm serious, Dante," Angela admitted. "I'm four to six weeks pregnant."

"Four to six weeks?" Dante replied, staring over at Angela, doing quick math inside his head and coming back with one month and two weeks, which would mean she got pregnant right before Alinna. "Ain't this a bitch?"

Pulling inside the motel parking lot, Angela parked and turned facing Dante. "Dante listen, I know we started things all wrong, but I want that to change. I'm up for a promotion for my lieutenant bars in another week. I don't want you to worry about anything and I'm going to make sure that you have nothing to worry about. Just promise me you'll be there for me and our child."

Shaking his head, Dante ran his left hand over his face, and then said, "Angela look, if this really my shorty you're supposedly carrying, I'ma take care of mines, but understand that this same Alinna chick you asking me about is my first priority, that's not going to change."

Upset at what she was hearing but smiling at having her own plans for Dante and herself, Angela leaned over to him, kissing his ear, and then licking the rim of his ears with her left hand moving over between his legs and gripping his manhood. She said, "Just make sure you take care of us and I'm happy."

Hearing Angela's words but really not paying them much attention, Dante sat thinking about Alinna and the child they were having together.

$ $ $

Pissed off while lying in their new queen size bed that she picked out for them while Vanessa and the other sat downstairs in the den watching some movie they ordered on Netflix, Alinna looked over at her cell phone wanting to call Dante, but refused herself for some reason she couldn't explain.

"Fuck him," Alinna said, climbing out of the bed and started toward the door just as Dante walked through causing her to stop mid-step.

Staring at Dante as he walked to the closet and stood pulling off his shirt, Alinna spoke first seeing that he wasn't going to say anything. "So you not gonna say nothing Dante? You just going to walk in here and not tell me where you been?"

"Not right now Alinna," Dante told her, walking naked to their bathroom, leaving his clothes in front of the closet.

Sucking her teeth, Alinna stormed off behind Dante while entering the bathroom just as he was stepping inside the standing shower.

Stripping naked without a thought, Alinna walked over to the glass shower door snatching it open stepping inside to find Dante facing the wall with his forehead laid against the wall while the water beat down on his back.

"What now Alinna?" Dante asked from his position facing the wall still.

Stepping up behind him only to jump back at feeling how cold the water was that was spraying from the showerhead, Alinna turned on the hot water then turned Dante to face her, reaching up taking his face in both her hands forcing him to look back at her. "Baby, what's wrong? This isn't about Wesley is it? Something else is bothering you."

"It's nothing Alinna," Dante told her, turning away from her only for her to force him back around.

"Dante, don't start lying to me, tell me what's wrong. I can see it on your face and your eyes. Tell me you're upset, what is it?"

Holding Alinna's eyes for a few minutes, Dante asked out of the blue, "Do you trust me?"

"What?" Alinna asked shocked and surprised. "What type of fucking question is that, Dante?"

"Just answer the question, Alinna," Dante told her in a calm voice that had Alinna staring at him in an odd way.

"Dante you know I trust you. I love you. Please tell me what's going on," Alinna told him beginning to worry now.

"Just know that no matter what ever happens in the future, I'm only for you and our shorty," Dante told her dropping his hand to her stomach. "I love you Alinna, I swear."

Unable to say anything else, Dante kissed her. Alinna allowed him to pick her up wrapping her arms and legs around him, feeling him position his manhood at the entrance of her womanhood she cried out while kissing him feeling Dante slid up inside her.

$ $ $

Lying in bed with Dante with his head laid on her chest while he slept, Alinna laid rubbing his hair wondering what happened to Dante, and why he was acting so weird and talking the way he was while they was in the shower.

Thinking and still trying to put together everything inside her head, Alinna found herself thinking back over the past few months since she and Dante began seeing each other intimately, noticing a few things more she thought back.

Focusing on Dante as he shifted positions wrapping his arm around her middle squeezing her tight then loosening his hold, Alinna bent her head down enough to kiss the top of his head then whispered, "What are you keeping from me, Dante?"

15

Continuing to deal with Dante and his mood swings and noticing the odd times he needed to disappear for long stretches of hours, Alinna gave up on asking him where he'd been or what he was doing, instead making decisions of her own.

Around the fifth month of her pregnancy, Alinna got an answer to what she wanted to know about Dante's whereabouts for those long hours he was away after receiving a phone call from Amber a few hours after Dante left.

"Yeah Amber, where are you?"

"Alinna look, I want you to sit down before I tell you where I'm at."

"Amber don't play with me, where the hell are you?"

"Alinna think about the…"

"Amber if I ask you again I promise after I deal with Dante and his shit, I will deal with you and your bullshit, now tell me, where is my man?"

Listening to Amber tell her what she was hearing, Alinna wasn't sure how she found the bed, but she was barely aware that she actually was sitting down and tears were running down her face.

After hanging up with Amber, Alinna wasn't sure how long she sat at the foot of the bed in deep thought when Dante walked in their bedroom.

Following him with her eyes as Dante moved around the bedroom not saying anything to her but mumbling to himself, Alinna grew tired of waiting and said, "Dante where the fuck have you been and I swear if you lie to me I will fuck you up this day. Answer me nigga."

Glancing over to Alinna as he headed towards their bathroom, Dante answered, saying back over his shoulder to Alinna, "Handling business, Alinna."

Standing to her feet before she realized that she even moved, Alinna stormed into the bathroom behind Dante catching him standing in front of the toilet pissing, she swung punching Dante directly in the mouth.

"Muthafucka, I told you not to lie to me," Dante heard Alinna yell after getting past the fact she punched him in the mouth, feeling blood as it ran down his bottom lip.

Licking his lip, Dante finished pissing, flushed the toilet, walked over to wash his hands, while ignoring the blood he saw dripping into the sink.

Drying off his hand's once he was done, Dante left the bathroom with Alinna still yelling and trailing him, unsure of what the fuck she was saying as he walked over to the dresser grabbing his burner, keys, and cell phone.

"Dante where the fuck you going now?" Alinna yelled grabbing Dante arm.

Looking back to Alinna meeting her eyes directly, Dante wasn't sure what the hell he said that caused Alinna to release her hold on him, but he simply walked out of the room and left the house.

$ $ $

Leaving the house in the Altima, heading nowhere in particular but driving around thinking, Dante was deep in thought when he pulled up to a red light besides a dark blue Impala recognizing the Chevy. He hit the car horn then lowered his window just as the passenger side window of the Impala slid down.

"Fuck you doing around this part of town?" Dante asked yelling from his car over to Vegas in the Impala.

"A lil business I was handling. What's good though, gangster? Where ya headed?"

"Get something to eat real quickly." Dante moved up just as the light changed to green.

"I'm gonna slide with ya. I'll follow you," Vegas told Dante, then let the window up.

Really not in the mood to be kicking it with anybody, Dante let it go and decided to pull inside the KFC on the left.

$ $ $

Worried that she may have went too far with putting her hand's on Dante, remembering the look on this face when he told her to let him go before he left the house, Alinna sat on the bed calling Dante's cell phone, but getting nothing but his voicemail.

Close to screaming after getting Dante's voicemail again, Alinna hung up and was just about to dial the number back when her cell phone rang back.

Watching as Amber called, Alinna answered, "Please tell me you're still following him, Amber."

"He's at the KFC, but you're not going to believe what I gotta tell you."

"What now"

"First, I found out who the bitch was that Dante was with, but that's half of what's important. What's important is the bitch is either fucking with Dante's ex-boy, Vegas or something else is going down because when Dante left her house I waited a few minutes and guess who I saw pull up? Vegas' ass."

"What happen?"

"The bitch and Vegas just stood outside talking by his car. But guess what, she's pregnant, Alinna."

Quiet for a moment praying that Dante wasn't the father of whoever this other bitch was, Alinna broke her silence. "Amber, get Dante's ass home. Go inside that KFC and tell him to get his ass home now."

$ $ $

"So what the hell are you doing on this side of town?" Vegas asked Dante once they sat down across from one another on the left side of KFC, overlooking the parking lot.

"Handling a little something as well," Dante answered as he pulled a chicken breast from the box. "What's good with you though? I ain't heard from you in a lil minute though."

"Just tryna live, my nigga," Vegas answered, and then asked, "Yo what's up with Alinna? You still kicking it with shorty?"

"Why the fuck you worried about it, nigga?" Amber said with much attitude as she walked up on the table with Dante and Vegas.

"What the fuck you doing here Amber?" Dante asked, surprised to see her.

"You slipping Dante," Amber told him shooting Vegas a nasty look, and then looking back to Dante. "Dante you need to get home. Alinna called me and she needs you home now."

"What's up?" Dante asked as he was standing from his seat.

"I'm not sure but we need to go," Amber told him grabbing Dante's arm pulling him away from the table.

Jogging out to his car as Amber ran and jumped in her Acura, Dante got his car door opened and got inside and then pulled out his cell phone. Turning on his cell phone as he was back out of the parking lot and driving away, Dante cursed under his breath seeing 11 missed calls.

Making it back to the house in under seven minutes, Dante swung the Altima in the driveway and around the front of the house, parking in the back of Dre's Avalanche.

Hopping out of his car, Dante caught a glimpse of Amber parking the Acura. Dante jogged up to the front door, snatching open the door.

"Alinna!" Dante yelled as he rushed into the house, yelling her name as Dre and Vanessa rushed out of the den and rose hurried from the kitchen to see what was going on.

"Yo fam, what's up?" Dante heard Dre call out as he was already running up the stairs.

"Dee, what's up braw?" Tony T asked as he rushed out in the hallway with his burner in hand, while Dante flew up the stairs on the top level.

Ignoring Tony T catching a glimpse of Harmony rushing out of her bedroom while putting on her shirt, Dante ran to his own bedroom with Alinna sitting on the bed smoking a joint with the T.V. running.

Looking around the bedroom seeing nothing but smelling the weed in the air, Dante sat down one of his Glocks he didn't remember pulling out, asking Alinna, "What the hell is going on? And what the hell are you fucking doing?"

Allowing Dante to snatch the joint from her hand, Alinna sat watching him smash out the joint then turn angrily facing her she smoke first, "Who the fuck is the pregnant bitch that you've been seeing behind my back, Dante?"

Caught off guard by her question, Dante looked to the bedroom door after hearing it close. He looked back to Alinna, seeing the expression on her face. "Alinna it's ..."

"Dante, if you lie to me right now I promise you I will put you in the hospital," Alinna interrupted, picking up her .380 from beside her left thigh and laying it on top of her lap while staring at Dante the whole time.

Ignoring the gun, Dante backed up against the wall and folded his arm across his chest staring back at Alinna. "Her name is Angela Perez."

"Is she pregnant from you?"

"Yes."

"So you cheated on me?" Alinna asked as tears of hurt and anger broke free.

"No, I didn't cheat on you," Dante replied, as he remained leaning against the wall staring at Alinna. "I met Angela before you and we never began seeing each other like that."

"Just tell me the truth Dante, do you love her? Please don't lie," Alinna begged him.

Laughing at hearing Alinna's question and seeing the look on her face at his laughing, Dante finally got out, "I wouldn't use the love word, and what I feel for her isn't in the same sentence as you shorty, believe me, it's not the same."

Telling Alinna everything from the first time Angela pulled him over and making her demands and explaining how they were able to get away with all the murders they had in the city, which was why he was happy they now handle business out of the state, Dante saw and hated the look that Alinna gave him when he admitted to having sex with Angela once after he and Alinna began seeing each other.

"How far along is she, Dante?" Alinna asked him as she was still pissed off, but more with the detective bitch who was impregnated by her man.

"She's a month and a few weeks ahead of you," Dante admitted.

"Do you know how she is able to keep up with your whereabouts or how she found out who I was?" Alinna asked him as she moved the .380 from her lap and climbed off the bed walking over to the dresser where Dante left the joint.

"I think she's having me followed, but I can never spot anyone undercover following me," Dante told her as he walked over to Alinna, taking the joint from her hand, and receiving a nasty look for it.

Rolling her eyes at him mumbling something in Spanish that Dante didn't catch, Alinna sat back down on the bed facing him. "She has Vegas following you, Dante."

"Vegas, what are you talking about?" Dante asked confused at what she was telling him.

Explaining to Dante how she had been having Amber follow him for the past two weeks and how Amber found out about Angela, but also found out that Vegas was also meeting up with Angela right behind him which had to be how she was able to keep up with him whenever he was inside the city, Alinna watched Dante's facial expression the whole time.

"That explains why the police bitch was over this way just now," Dante said once Alinna finished talking. "I caught up with his ass a few blocks from here at the light; he said he was handling some business."

"I bet he was handling business – police business," Alinna replied and then asked, "What are we going to do about Angela, Dante?"

"I know you may not want to hear this, but we may need her in the future. She's getting a promotion and she may be of use for us once things start growing in business, and she is carrying my shorty," Dante explained.

"How the fuck you know that it's your fucking baby?" Alinna yelled angrily from the thought of hearing about somebody else having Dante baby.

Walking from the wall where he was leaning, Dante sat next to Alinna as she was crying with a pissed off expression on her face, Dante wiped her face. Then he said, "Shorty, I know you're heated but what's done is done. I'll get a blood test to make sure, but tell me now what you want to do before we go any further."

Staring at Dante a few minutes, Alinna sighed deeply as she learned over against him, wrapping her arms saying, "I love you Dante, but please don't make me kill you for cheating on me with anybody."

"Relax shorty, I don't want nobody else," Dante told her wrapping his arms around her, kissing Alinna on top of her head.

16

After Angela and Alinna had their babies – Alinna a boy, while Angela had a little girl, Dante was able to split his time between both his kids after finding out that Mya Blackwell was his actual daughter.

Once Alinna got back in the vibe of things and Angela got back to work, business began picking up to a level where Alinna broke down and gave her girls a different location that Dante, Dre, Tony T, and Wesley ensured was available to them without any problems.

With Amber, Harmony, Vanessa, and Wesley running their new locations, building a crew that ran the trap house only noticing that business was getting bigger and more money and customers were coming in, Dante, Dre, and Tony T went back to work making trips out to West Virginia and Tennessee returning home with nine bricks of coke, ten pounds of weed, and a little over ten thousand pills.

Stopping by Angela's house to see Mya one Saturday morning and seeing a dark blue Jeep Cherokee parked in the driveway behind Angela's car, Dante parked the new matted out black Range Rover that Alinna had bought him.

Climbing from the Range Rover and walking around the front end of the SUV just as his cell phone went off, Dante pulled out his cell phone seeing Alinna calling, he answered, "Yeah baby, what's up?"

"Where are you?"

"Seeing Mya," Dante answered as he knocked on the door of Angela's house. "What's up?"

"I need you to pick up some medicine for D.J. at the CVS," Dante heard Alinna tell him just as the front door opened and a Spanish dude walked in through the front door to Angela's house with Mya in his arms.

"Alinna let me hit you back," Dante told her, hanging up the phone before Alinna could respond while starting hard at the Spanish guy holding his daughter.

"Yeah, you here to …"

"Geno, who's at the door," Angela asked as she walked up only to see Dante and broke out a smile. "Hi baby, why didn't you call and tell me you were coming?"

"Who's he and what's wrong with this picture?" Dante asked nodding towards the Spanish guy.

Looking from Dante to Geno then noticing what had Dante's handsome face all balled up, Angela took Mya from Geno, and then introduced the two of them. "Dante this is my brother Geno, Geno this is Mya's father, Dante I told you about."

"What's up man?" Dante heard Geno say with a thick Spanish accent, ignoring the guy as he took Mya from Angela then walking into the house.

Walking directly into the front room, Dante sat down onto the sofa with Mya, playing with her just as Angela came walking into the front room a few minutes later sitting down beside him. "For the future, I don't want different men holding my daughter, Angela."

Knowing better than to argue with him about his daughter, Angela simply agreed and then asked, "Are you hungry?"

"Naw I'm good but you can get me something to drink though," Dante told her cutting his eyes over to Angela as she stood up beside him. Walking off, he couldn't help but notice that just as Alinna having his baby did justice for Angela's body it did hers as well.

Focusing back to his daughter, Dante took the bottle of Corona that Angela handed to him noticing that she now kept a supply of Coronas since finding out it was the only beer he drank.

"Dante, I need to talk to you," Angela told him as she sat back next to him leaving against Dante.

"I'm listening," Dante replied, noticing Angela's position, but allowing it for the moment.

"I'm supposed to go out of town on business next week. I need you to watch Mya until I get back."

"How long you going to be gone?"

"You gonna miss me?"

"Answer the question Angela

"Just a week then I'm coming back. I'm supposed to pick up a prisoner and fly him back here from New Jersey."

"Call me and let me know when you're back," Dante told her just as his cell phone went off again.

Seeing Tony T calling, Dante answered, "What's good T?"

"Braw where you at?"

"Seeing Mya, why?"

"We're all at the hospital. Vanessa's about to have her baby and Dre's asking about you. Ya lady on her way."

"What hospital y'all at?"

"Jackson."

"Alright, I'm on my way now."

Hanging up the phone, Dante gave Mya to Angela only to hear her ask, "Dante, where are you going? What happened?"

"Dre's girlfriend is having her baby," Dante told her kissing his daughter, then pulling out a large bankroll. He peeled off $500 and handed it to Angela saying, "I'll call you later."

$ $ $

Leaving Angela's house and pulling into Jackson Memorial Hospital twenty minutes later, Dante found a parking space and even though he didn't like it. He left both of his burners inside the Range Rover then jogged through the parking lot to the front door of the hospital.

Not bothering with stopping at the desk for information, Dante pulled out his phone and called Tony T getting the information on where they were.

Five minutes later, stepping out of the elevator on the third floor, Dante jogged down the end of the hall, made a left and spotted Tony T, Harmony, Amber, and Wesley as well as Alinna who was talking to Amber and Harmony.

"What's up y'all?" Dante asked as he walked up on the group.

"Baby," Alinna cried, walking up to Dante hugging and kissing him.

"Where's Dre and Vanessa?" Dante asked looking at Alinna and Tony T.

"They just took her inside," Alinna answered him. "They've been there a little over five minutes now."

"Braw, you should've seen Dre. Homeboy looked as if he was about to lose it," Tony T said jokingly.

"Shut up, Tony," Harmony told him, elbowing Tony T in his side.

"I wanna see how you act when I have your baby."

"What do you mean *when*?" Tony T asked as he began to panic. "You pregnant women?"

Shaking his head at Tony T and Harmony, Dante looked to Wesley hearing him call his name getting his attention. "What's up Wesley?"

"What's going on, brethren? We need to talk a second, Rastaman," Wesley told Dante nodding for Dante to step to the side with him.

"What's good Wesley?" Dante asked once he and Wesley stood away from the others.

"Member the blood clot rude boy you tell me about?"

"Yeah what about him?"

"Pulling out a photo from his pocket, Wesley handed the picture over to Dante. "Is this him?"

Looking at the photo Dante instantly recognized Vegas even though it was a picture of his head after it was amputated from his body.

Slowly smiling looking back to Wesley, Dante asked, "This your work?"

Nodding his head that it was with a small smile on his lips, Wesley dapped up with Dante once Dante held up his fist showing respect and a show of love.

$ $ $

Vanessa gave birth to a healthy baby boy. She and Dre named him Andre Payne Jr. Vanessa was then moved to her own room where Alinna and the others was allowed to visit her.

"How you feeling, girl?" Vanessa asked, cursing the others laughing.

"Here we go Vanessa," is what the others heard just as the nurse came in pushing a nursery bed into the room.

Smiling at seeing her son and watching as the nurse picked him up from his bed, Vanessa reached out taking her son smiling down at her.

"He looks like you and Dre," Dante spoke up as he stood across from Dre on the other side of Vanessa's bed.

"That means my little nigga is handsome just like his daddy," Dre said, smiling as he bent down and kissed first Vanessa then his son's head.

Spending some time with Vanessa until the nurse announced that Vanessa and the baby needed to rest and that everybody needed to leave, Dre kissed Vanessa and his son again, and then handed Vanessa her cell phone telling her to call if she needed anything.

After the other girls left and said their goodbyes, everyone else left the room. Dante fell asleep with Dre smiling at his boy. "How does it feel bro?"

Shaking his head and smiling, Dre answered, "I'm still trying to get my head right over it all, but I do know one thing – it's time that we turn it up because ain't no fucking way my son will want anything else, you feel me fam?"

Dapping with his best friend, Dante answered him saying, "Don't even worry braw, everything's gonna be good."

17

Three weeks after Vanessa had the baby and released to go home, Dante received a call from Angela telling him to meet her at the Denny's on 27th and 199th so they could talk.

Leaving the house and an upset Alinna, Dante pulled into Denny's twenty minutes later. Finding a spot to park, he climbed out of the Range Rover and headed into the restaurant.

Seeing Angela and his daughter as soon as he walked in the Denny's, Dante walked over smiling at his daughter who spotting him and began whining and reaching for him.

"What's up Angela?" Dante asked, taking Mya from her and then sitting down. "What's so important you had to get me out of my house at this hour?"

"Dante, I've got a problem I need you to help me."

"What problem?"

"It's my new captain, I'm about to be under investigation."

"Investigation? For what?" Dante asked, raising his eyes from his little girl looking at Angela.

Telling Dante about the problem she was having with her new captain with him flirting and asking her out and even going as far as feeling on her, which lead her to punch him in the mouth; the captain took it as a personal issue and turned it into a work issue. Angela cried angrily as she spoke.

"You still haven't told me what you being investigated for, Angela," Dante told her.

"He knows you're Mya's father and he trying to connect you with me. He wants us both arrested, Dante," Angela told him getting more upset.

"Arrested? For what?" Dante asked confused.

"He knows about the Narcotics Sergeant who was murdered by Alinna. He found out that Miguel was working for your girlfriend and he knows that Alinna and her friends are becoming one, if not *the* largest drug suppliers in the city, and it's well known that you, Andre, and Tony T are backing them.

"So what's the problem?" Dante asked her, "What's he waiting on? Why hasn't he sent anyone after us yet if he knows all of this?"

"Because he's waiting to get us all at once. He thinks that we all work together," Angela explained.

Nodding his head slowly, Dante said after a minute, "Tell me everything you got on this guy."

$ $ $

Returning to the house two hours later, Dante parked the Range Rover in the garage and went through the side door into the kitchen.

Heading up stairs, Dante made it halfway to his bedroom hearing Alinna's voice, walking into the room only to see Alinna and Vanessa seated at the foot of the bed talking with each other.

"I'll talk to you later," Vanessa told Alinna, standing up and kissing Dante on the cheek saying, "Hey big braw."

Smiling as she watched Vanessa leave, Alinna looked to Dante as she stopped next to the baby bed checking on his son. "What did Angela want?"

"We gotta problem," Dante replied walking away from his son day bed pulling off his shirt then sitting down on his side of the bed.

Once Dante undressed and climbed into bed, Alinna crawled into bed with him, curling up next to him laying her head on his chest. "Tell me what happened."

Breaking down the whole story to Alinna that Angela told him about Captain Whitehead, Dante finished his story only to say, "I'm gonna deal with his ass real soon."

"What's your plan?" Alinna asked him as she ran her left hand up and down his mid-section.

"I'm still putting it together," Dante told her as he started at the ceiling. "It's gonna have to be soon though."

$ $ $

Leaving the house again later that morning, Dante drove his old Nissan Altima and parked two houses across the street from the address Angela gave him.

Seeing the heavyset middle aged white man in his police uniform with the noticeable captain bars that shined on his collar, Dante sat watching Captain Whitehead kiss his wife goodbye then walked out to the black and chrome Lincoln Town Car.

Starting up the Nissan Altima once Captain Whitehead back the town car out of the driveway and drove away, Dante pulled off behind him driving right pass the captain's home.

Keeping a short distance away following it from the neighborhood, Dante pulled the Nissan up alongside of the town car at the stoplight a block away from where the captain lived.

Changing his plan at seeing the perfect opportunity with Captain Whitehead, he took out his cell phone and with the street nearly empty at this hour of the morning, Dante put the Altima in park then calmly opened his car door climbing out of the driver's seat and pulled out his Glock from the front of his jeans as Captain Whitehead was turning his head in his direction.

Boom! Boom! Boom! Boom!

Dumping a full clip into Captain Whitehead, Dante turned and climbed back into his Altima, and took one last look over to Captain Whitehead as the fat man laid slumped dead against the steering wheel driving off, Dante made a U-turn and simply drove away.

$ $ $

Getting rid of the Nissan Altima, Dante called and had Dre pick him up from the Burger King on 199th and 441st standing outside smoking a joint he took from Alinna before leaving the house earlier.

Hearing his cell phone wake up and ringing in his pocket, Dante got the phone out seeing Angela calling. He answered, "Yeah Angela."

"Dante where are you?" Angela asked sounding excited.

"Waiting for Dre," Dante answered her and then said, "If you're about to do some talking just wait till I get over there. Dre's gonna be here in a minute."

"Just tell me you're okay."

"I'm good Angela."

"Dante, I love you. I love you so much, baby."

"Yeah, I hear you," Dante replied hanging up the phone and shaking his head.

Once Dre's Land Rover pulled inside the Burger King ten minutes later after Dante hung up with Angela, he walked around to the passenger side and got in.

"What's up, fam?" Dre said dapping up with Dante after he got in the SUV

"What's good, braw?" Dante replied and then said, "Roll through Angela's spot real quick. She wanna holla at me."

"Everything good with Mya?" Dre asked him.

"Yeah, she just wanna holla about something else," Dante explained.

"What happened with your ride?" Dre asked as he drove away from the Burger King.

Telling Dre the whole conversation with Angela about Captain Whitehead and his plot to set them all up, Dante finished explaining and explained how they would have to lay back for a little while as Dre pulled in front of Angela's house just as she was stepping out the front door talking to Mya's babysitter.

"Hold up a second," Dante told Dre as he climbed from the Land Rover.

Heading up the walkway as Angela walked out to meet him, Dante crossed the front yard as Angela asked him, "Why didn't you tell me when you were planning to do this Dante?"

"Did it matter?" he asked as he walked around and climbed inside the passenger of Angela's ride.

Tossing her bags onto the backseat then climbing inside the driver's seat, Angela shut the car door, cranked up the engine, and looked to Dante saying, "It's all over the news what you did, and you must have hit him with every bullet in your magazine. I've already received over twenty calls since I'm next in position behind Captain Whitehead."

"Let me know what's going on," Dante told her and climbed out of the car when Angela called his name.

Turning back to see what she wanted only for Angela to lean over and kiss him on the lips, Dante was just about to push her away but found himself returning the kiss.

Breaking the kiss, Dante saw the expression on her face, and said, "Call me later and let me know what's going on."

"I love you, Dante," he heard her call out as he climbed from the car, shutting the door behind him.

$ $ $

Once Dre pulled off and parked in their front yard, Dante and Dre saw Harmony's new Audi go flying past them, leaving the house in a hurry.

After Dre parked his Land Rover inside the garage, Dante climbed out from the SUV just as his cell phone rang.

Looking at the phone seeing once he took it out his pocket, Dante answered, "What's up, shorty?"

"Dante, where are you?" Alinna asked after hearing Dante voice.

"I'm walking in the house now," Dante answered, receiving a smile from Rose as he and Dre entered the house through the kitchen.

Hearing the phone hang up in his ear, Dante looked at the screen and seeing that Alinna actually hung up on him. He shook his head.

"Dante, are you and Andre eating breakfast?" Rose asked looking from Dante to Dre then back.

"Yeah, you can hook something up," Dante answered leaving the kitchen and hearing Dre telling Rose exactly what he wanted. Making it halfway up the stairs as Alinna, D.J. walked up on him.

"Where the hell have you been, Dante?"

"Handling business," he told Alinna, taking his son out of Alinna's arms.

"What business?"

"What's up with you?"

"I'm wondering why is it when I wake up you're not in bed or even in the house? What business did you need to handle?"

"I told you about it last night," Dante told her and then asked, "What are you tripping about now?"

Staring up at Dante a moment, Alinna never had a chance to respond as Vanessa and Amber came downstairs.

"A, you ready?' Amber asked, noticing Alinna's facial expression cutting her eyes over to Vanessa, seeing her girl noticed Alinna expression also.

Rolling her eyes at Dante, Alinna started down the stairs again calling for both Vanessa and Amber to come on so they can leave.

18

"**A**linna, are you okay?" Vanessa asked her girl as they drove away from the time house. Driving in Alinna's new BMW 325I, she glanced back and forth from the road back over to Alinna. Hearing Vanessa and staring out of her window from the passenger seat, Alinna responded after a minute passed. "I think something's up with that bitch Angela."

"You mean Dante's daughters mom?" Amber asked from the backseat.

"Yeah, that bitch," Alinna answered nastily.

"I thought everything was alright with you and Dante on that level," Vanessa added.

"I was," Alinna replied and looked to Vanessa saying, "This bitch called Dante at twelve something in the morning about some problem he told me about after he got home. Then his ass was gone again when I woke up. When I asked him where he had been he said some mess about taking care of business."

"You know how that man is better than all of us. He's always handling something," Amber spoke up.

"What's wrong with him taking care of a problem?" Vanessa asked.

"I do not care about Dante handling his business. What I do care about is my man coming home smelling like some other bitch. That's what the problem is," Alinna stated, with her anger heard through her voice. Turning her attention back out of the window Vanessa and Amber sat quietly. Alinna stared out the window not seeing anything and thinking about how she could get to the bottom of this problem.

$ $ $

Turning down the block where Harmony's trap house was after calling her worker's, Tony T slowed his Aston Martin in front of the trap house, but sat looking out of the tinted passenger window for a brief moment, trying to understand what he was seeing.

Parking the Aston Martin behind the black Escalade that was also parked out front of the trap house, Tony T hopped out only to hear Harmony yelling at two dudes who stood facing off with Harmony and her three workers.

"Is there a problem here?" Tony T asked, walking up on the group with his burner in his right fist, stopping beside Harmony. "Harmony, what's good?

"These two bitch ass niggas can't understand that I don't care who the fuck they work for. My price won't lower for them, him, or whoever the fuck ..." Harmony said as she mean-mugged the two guy's that were standing in front of her.

"You got your heat out like your planning on using it, homie," one of the two dudes said, directing his attention on Tony T. Slowly smiling at the guy, Tony T decided to not say anything on it and ignored his statement. Instead he asked, "Who you niggas work for?"

"Who are you supposed to be?" the other guy asked Tony T looking him up and down. Shaking his head and smiling, Tony T called Harmony in close and asked, "Baby, what's up? We doing business or what?

"Fuck them niggas and the bitch nigga they work for, ain't no business here for them," Harmony stated with attitude.

"Alright niggas, y'all ran out of time so y'all need to be gone by the time I finish talking or I'ma make sure one if not both of you go back to your boss holding onto your own insides in."

"You mothafucka!"

BOOM!

"What the fuck?" one of the guys yelled after seeing his boy get shot in the stomach, now laying on the ground holding his guts in pain.

"That's one, you got a choice," Tony T told the guy staring at him while maintaining a smirk on his face.

Watching the other guy help his homeboy up and out to the Escalade, Harmony shook her after the truck pulled off. Tony T asked, "Who the fuck were they?"

"I don't know," Harmony answered and then said, "They supposedly work for some nigga named Raul. They're not even from here. They're supposed to be from Orlando."

"What are they trying to get?" Tony T asked as he tucked his gun in back into his jeans.

"Supposedly whoever this Raul nigga is, he wanted five bricks and sent me some bullshit message about the twelve grand and it wasn't negotiable."

"I know the price is nineteen a piece, but I thought you let him go for 12 when they buy four or better?" Tony T said.

"Nah, I didn't like the vibe they gave me and I don't like this Raul dude sending people to give me a message as if he is somebody on a whole other level.

"Yeah, I hear you," Tony T said, and then added, "Just keep your eyes open and let me know if you got any more problems."

"Aww you worried about me?" Harmony asked, smiling as she wrapped her arm around Tony's neck.

Gripping Harmony's thick ass, he replied, "I know you can handle whatever but, let me know anyway."

"Yes, Daddy," Harmony replied, leaning into Tony T kissing his cheek only to scream when he gave her a slap on her butt.

"Now where's my weed you promised me?" Tony T asked grinning.

$ $ $

Hearing about the murder of Captain Ben Whitehead all over the streets and even on the radio, Alinna found herself splitting her focus from business and news on the Captain. The last update was that Sergeant Angela Perez would be taking over for Captain Whitehead.

"So that's what this is all about?" Alinna said aloud, talking to herself as she and Vanessa drove off from the dropping off Amber with Wesley to get her car from the shop.

"What, what was about?" Vanessa asked, glancing over to Alinna.

"That's what Angela needed Dante for; she used him to get another promotion at the police station."

"So you think she lied to Dante and had him kill this Whitehead guy just to take his spot?"

"She probably wasn't lying completely, but I don't think this Whitehead guy knew everything she said he knew. I think she had added more to it so Dante would go after the guy; she knows how Dante is, just as much as I know."

"Why do I have the feeling you are thinking something else, Alinna?"

Quiet for a moment, Alinna replied, "I think she is after Dante."

"After him how?" Vanessa asked

"She is gonna use her position to give Dante the freedom to do whatever he wants and in return he will have to turn away from me."

"Now you know Dante is crazy about you. You gave that boy his first son."

"Yeah but she gave him his first child," Alinna replied just as her phone went off. Pulling her phone from her purse, Alinna saw that it was one of her major buyer's calling.

"What's up Rick?" she answered.

"What's up Alinna? You too busy to holla at a nigga doing your queen-pin thing or what?"

"I got time for you boo, talk to me."

"Check this out, I got a dude from outta town who's trying to do business with you, but he's trying to cook up some pot sew. He wanna get like 10 onions."

"Okay, you know this dude, Rick?"

"Real talk. I have heard of him Alinna ... but, he's been missing off the maps for some months now."

"So are you putting your word in for this guy that he will do good business?"

"Alinna ... look."

"Just answer the question, yes or no?"

"Alright, yeah," Rick hesitated

"Alright. You know if shit's not right with this guy you're sending me that I will need to have Dante clean up and then come see you."

"Damn, I thought we were cool. You gonna send that crazy ass dude after me?" Rick said baffled.

"It's business, Rick," Alinna told him. "What's this guy's name?"

"He goes by Fish Man."

"Fish what?" Alinna asked with sarcasm as if she hadn't heard Rick correctly.

"Fish Man, like with the scales and what not."

"Oh, okay ... Fish Man. Send me his number and I will text him tonight," Alinna said.

$ $ $

Hearing his phone go off as he and his son laid sleeping together, Dante reached back behind him and answered, "Yeah?"

183

"Hi baby, you busy?"

"What's up Angela?" he asked, looking down at his son after hearing D.J. moan while rolling over onto his side.

"I am just calling like you told me to, but guess what?"

"Tell me."

"They are promoting me this Friday. I won't work on the streets anymore and it will be a desk job from now on."

"Where are you?"

"Out in my car in the parking lot, why?" Angela responded

"I thought you were inside the station talking to me."

"Dante come on, you mean the world to me, and you are the father of our daughter. I am really careful when it comes to anything to protect you. I love you."

"Yeah I hear you," Dante replied. "What time do you get off?"

"I'm not sure. I will call you when I find out," Angela told him. "Are you coming to see me and Mya tonight?"

"Just call me when you get off, Angela," Dante told her, hanging up the phone and shaking his head.

$ $ $

Finishing her business runs, Alinna rode with Vanessa to her trap house to drop off more work with her crew. Remembering Fish Man that Rick had told her about, she went through her phone to find his number. Listening to the line ringing as she called whoever this Fish Man was, Alinna nodded her head to Vanessa after she said she would be right back.

"Who's this?" Alinna heard a heavy country sounding voice answer.

"I am calling for whoever Fish Man is," Alinna replied.

"You the chick I have been hearing about, the one that's supposed to have the city locked down?"

Ignoring the comment Alinna said, "Rick tells me you are looking to connect on a business level. Is that correct?"

"So it's true then?"

"Is what true?" she asked.

"You having shit on lock in the city."

"Look Fish Man or whatever, if you are looking to discuss history or my background wait for the autobiography. What the fuck you gonna do?"

"Ooh feisty," he replied. "I am sure Rick told you I am looking for ten k ..."

"He told me," she said abruptly interrupting his speaking. "We can discuss facts in person and not on the phone."

"Fine, when can we meet?" Alinna gave Fish Man a time and a location for their meeting and hung up, just as Vanessa was getting back into the car.

19

Getting into it with some of Raul's guys again and hearing about the shootout at the trap house, Harmony did as she was told and notified Tony T, and also put Alinna up on what was going on.

"Harmony, what's up?" Dante asked catching Harmony inside the den while watching TV, while feeding Vanessa's son a bottle. Looking over to Dante and seeing the expression on his face, Harmony went straight into explaining what she knew. "I am not sure who this Raul guy is, but a few days ago he sent some guys over to my spot, demanding work at a price that he set for himself. When I told his boys that I wasn't doing business with them, they started talking crazy. Tony T drove up and saw what was going on. He shot one of them in the stomach and had the other guy carry him off the front yard."

"So now this Raul clown is trying to get back then after he sent his boys to the trap and shot it up?" Dante asked.

Nodding her head, Harmony asked, "What are you planning on doing, Dante?"

"I'll let you know when I find out who this Raul nigga is," Dante told Harmony, turning and walking out of the den. Dante pulled out his phone and called Wesley.

"Who's dis?" Wesley answered in the middle of a ring.

"Where you at? This Dante."

"What's good brother?"

"I need to take care of something for me. Where you at?"

"Me at me spot mon."

"I'ma be there is a few minutes," Dante told Wesley and then hung up. Using the Kawasaki Ninja, Dante took off from the house flying up the street past Alinna's BMW.

$ $ $

Seeing Dante as he flew by her on his bike, Alinna almost turned her car around and followed him. She knew that she couldn't keep up with him on that bike though so it would have been pointless. Continuing on to her house, she parked around back near the garage and grabbed her shopping bag.

Once inside the house seeing that her girls were there, she nodded to the older women and started for the stairs, but saw that Harmony and baby Andre were in the den. "Hey, what's up?" Harmony asked, seeing Alinna when she walked into the den. "What did you do today? You go shopping?"

"Yeah, I got D.J. some new clothes his ass already too big for the ones I just bought him a couple weeks ago," she said, sitting down on the couch.

"You just missed your man, he literally just left."

"He say where he was going?" Alinna asked.

"You know Dante doesn't tell no one where he is ass is at. He just said he would tell me his plan after he found out who Raul is."

"Speaking of finding out who someone is, I want you ready for tomorrow night. I am supposed to meet with this guy that calls himself Fish Man. He's thinking about buying ten keys of coke, but he is out of town."

"How did you meet him?" questioned Harmony

"Another one of my customers who's a large scale buyer came to me about the guy."

"What time tomorrow?"

"Nine," Alinna answered as both Amber and Vanessa walked into the room.

$ $ $

Pulling up into the driveway parking her car, Angela got her phone out to call Dante.

"Yeah Angela, what's up?" Dante answered.

"Dante, where are you?" she asked.

"Handling some business."

"I am at home. I need you to come by here and I have to be back to work soon."

"What's going on?"

"Baby, can you please just come? I really need you Dante."

Quiet for a moment Dante said, "Give me fifteen minutes."

Hearing Dante then hang up, she smiled as she got out of the car and headed up to the front door. Opening the door to her babysitter, Jennifer walked from the backroom. "Ms. Perez, you are home early," Jennifer greeted speaking only Spanish.

Angela replied while heading to her room, "I will only be home for a moment. Maya's father is on his way and will be here soon. Let him in and send him to my bedroom."

$ $ $

Wesley contacted his information source to help him find out who Raul was. "Hello," a woman answered.

"Rachel, this is Wesley."

"Hey Wesley, what's up?"

"I need some information from ya."

"Okay, you know what I charge."

"Don't ya worry none. You get paid well for the help you give girl. You get paid extra this time."

"Now that's what I'm talking about. What you wanna know?"

"I need to find out who the rude boy is. He call himself Raul. Me need to know dis fast."

"I will call you as soon as I find out who he is."

Hanging up the phone, Wesley rubbed his hands together, smiling in anticipation and envisioning what might happen to this Raul guy when they find out who he is.

$ $ $

Seeing both Jennifer and Angela's car parked outside, Dante parked his ninja behind Jennifer's Honda Accord. Dante climbed off the bike, took his helmet off, and started for the front door. Just as he began to knock, the door opened for him almost immediately by the smiling babysitter.

Dante stepped inside and Jennifer told him in a heavy accent as best she could, "Angela is in the back." Heading to the back stopping first to see his daughter in her room fast asleep. Dante kissed his little girl and then walked over to Angela's closed bedroom door and knocked.

"It's open ..." Angela called from inside the bedroom, opening the bedroom door. Dante stepped in and shut the door behind him. To his right he could see Angela stepping from out of the master bathroom in nothing but a black thong and a matching bra.

"Do you like papi?" Angela asked as she walked over to him and pressing her body against his. Dante grabbed her by her small waist and pushed her a step back from him so there bodies were no longer touching. "I need you papi," Angela whined.

"Angela chill," Dante said almost looking toward the ceiling and not at her.

"Dante, I have faithfully waited for you. I have given you a beautiful daughter and I refuse every other guy that tries to talk to me because I belong to you." Angela brought herself closer to him and unzipped his jeans. "I know how you feel about Alinna, but whether you're willing to admit it or not, I am just as much your woman as she is. Please don't leave me by myself when you know I love you."

Getting Dante's jeans open and pulling them down, she reached her hand into his boxer's, then gripped Dante's manhood that was semi-hard for her already. Holding his eye's with hers, she lowered herself to a squatting position in front of him. Angela held up his dick and slowly licked from the base, all the way up to his fathead, as she came back down covering his dick with her mouth as she sucked it down. She smiled hearing her baby daddy let out a moan for her.

$ $ $

Knowing he was dead wrong but caught up in the moment as he slammed in and out of Angela, he switched her into different positions. Watching her expression's each time she came all over his dick and feeling the pressure of her climax each time, Dante ignored his own nut, slowing down or stopping each time if felt like he was going to explode. Getting Angela to beg him with tears running down her face as she looked back at him over her shoulder as he slammed deep up into her from the back, he watched her 41-inch ass jump and shake each time that he made contact. Dante gave into her cry, switching her onto her back and positioning himself between her legs as she wrapped her legs around his waist still crying out to him to cum for her.

Feeling on edge of exploding, Dante went to pull out and cum on her stomach. When she pulled him deeper inside of her with both legs she cried out she was cumming again just as he exploded, shooting his load deep inside of her.

Breathing hard as he laid on top of Angela while she held him tight, Dante caught his breath and pushed up off of her. Staring down at her and seeing how unbelievably cute she looked Dante said, "You better be on birth control girl."

"I'm not, so what?" she responded, seeing Dante's expression change she quickly added. "I am playing with you papi, I am. I don't want any more of your babies," she laughed as he looked at her crazy shaking his head like yeah right.

Dante laid beside her on the bed only to have Angela a turn towards him laying her head in his arms.

"Dante, I love you," Angela said to him

"Yeah I know Angela," was his reply

"You do?" Angela asked him smiling and sitting up to fully stare into his eyes.

"With how tight you just felt, I know you ain't been messing around, but you know I am leaving."

"Baby, I already know," Angela told Dante cutting him off. "I won't ask you to leave Alinna because I know you never will, but I will ask you to make time for us. We are your family too and your daughter and I both love you. Give us that much ..."

Sighing and shaking his head Dante ran his hand over her face and then said, "Alright Angela. I will give you that much." She leaned into him and kissed him.

20

Riding inside the passenger seat of Dre's Land Rover while Vanessa drove and Amber and Harmony sat in the backseat talking, Alinna was barely aware of what any of them were talking about. All she could think of was Dante.

"Alinna, are you alright girl?" Vanessa asked, noticing her staring off into the distance.

Losing her train of thought, Alinna looked over to Vanessa saying, "Yeah I'm fine girl. Just thinking about Dante's ass."

"He still not talking?"

"Yeah, he's talking but I got an odd feeling."

"What's that mean?"

"Like, same stuff something's up with him and that bitch, Angela. All of a sudden she been calling a lot more."

"Ask him about it."

"I want to, but I know I'm not gonna get nothing answered. If anything it will cause a fight between us."

"Yeah, well how about after this deal you guys take a trip? You, Dante, and D.J. It might do you good to have some time away with the boys," Vanessa said, knowing the possibility of something extra between Dante and Angela wouldn't be a shock but trying to soothe her girl.

"That might actually work. I will have to talk to him and see what he says, but only after we get done with this Fish Man fool," Alinna said, getting her mind back into business mode.

Once Vanessa pulled into the I.H.O.P. that Alinna had set as the meeting place, she immediately noticed the pearl white Escalade with two guys posted besides the truck smoking. Alinna, Amber, Vanessa, and Harmony all got out of the Land Rover as soon as Vanessa parked.

Glancing to her left as she and her girl's started toward the front entrance of the restaurant, Alinna caught the looks that the two guys were giving her and the crew.

Once inside, Alinna waved off the I.H.O.P. hostess, having seen the group of guys staring at her. She led them to the five men sitting together who were already seated.

"Fish Man?" Alinna called looking to the table of men.

One man spoke up. "You must be Alinna? I recognize that sexy voice," she recognized his country accent. The red-skinned man who had spoken up looked her up and down.

Alinna ignored the way he looked at her and said, "How about you tell your boy's here to let us sit?"

"Y'all heard the lady, move," Fish Man directed his crew.

Once two of his guy's got up and made room, Alinna and Vanessa sat down with Fish Man. Alinna began, "Here is the deal, I let my key's go for nineteen a piece, but because you trying to get twelve, I will do you a favor and let them go for twelve a key."

"Do I know you from somewhere?" Fish Man questioned Alinna.

"Did you hear what I just said?" Alinna asked looking at the man as if he was crazy.

"That's it!" Fish Man continued while snapping his fingers together and smiling. "You used to get your supply from that boy Kenny K! Sometime back, I remember you and your friend here. You two would swing by his spot and get weed from him. Well I'll be damned, look at y'all girls now."

Not liking what she was hearing, Alinna simply stood up from her seat and was followed by the rest of the girls who all stood as well.

"What's up, where you going?" Fish Man held his hands in the air as he watched them all walk away.

Making it back outside and seeing the same two guy's standing there as they were before, Alinna and the girls walked right by and headed straight for the Land Rover when they heard, "Hey! Where the fuck you bitches going?

Business ain't done!" Stopping and looking back over her shoulder, Fish Man stood there with his boys.

Alinna turned around facing the five guys and said, "Because I think you're too stupid to realize whose city you're in, I'll let the bitch comment go. As far as business, there will be no business."

"You mean to tell me you hoes..." Fish Man started only to get interrupted.

"What was that you just said homeboy?" Fish Man heard looking to his right at the pearl white Escalade. Seeing a light brown-skinned guy and a dark-skinned guy standing up against the hood of the truck, staring at him.

"Motherfucker, who the hell are you?" Fish Man said spitting as he forced the words out with his country accent. "Matter of fact, fuck this," Fish Man finished.

Seeing Fish Man motion to the guy's standing with him, Alinna looked over to Dante. Hearing him whistle, Dre and Tony T stepped out from the truck with them two A-R 15s.

"What the fuck is this?" Fish Man asked, looking from the guys with assault rifles who were now calmly leaning against the truck as well back to Alinna and the girls.

"You brought these niggers with you?" Fish Man questioned.

"Like I said before," Alinna started with a smile now on her face. "You're not in your city anymore. This is my city and I said we ain't doing business ... bitch." Seeing the look on his face as she, Vanessa, Amber, and Harmony all turned away. Laughing, Alinna continued to the car leaving Fish Man standing there.

$ $ $

Trailing behind Alinna after everyone had settled down, Dante drove deep in thought when his phone rang. 'Wesley,' it read. Turning down the music, he answered breaking his racing thoughts, "What up Wesley?"

"Brethren, me got info on blood clot boy you was needing. Him name is Raul Martinez from Orlando. That mon got em self two traps. One on dee nort side and one dem out in the city."

"You ain't find out where he stays?" Dante questioned.

"Nah, me people no find nothing. Dem says don't nobody know where blood clot lay him head. He real quiet, but we know how to find em."

"Alright, true." Dante hung up, and dialed Angela. Nodding his head as another plan came to him.

"Captain Perez," Angela answered.

"It's me," said Dante.

"Hold on please, sir," Angela replied and remained silent for a few minutes.

"Hi, baby!" she said when she returned to the line. "I was thinking of you. What's up?"

"I need a favor."

"What is it?"

"I have the spots I wanted you to have watched for me but I need them watched by a motherfucker that work for you and not me."

"I understand, what's going on?" she asked concerned.

"I will explain later."

"Okay, are you coming over tonight?"

"Just call me when you get off work."

"I love you."

"I know," Dante replied as he hung up the phone.

$ $ $

When everyone made it back to the house, both crews gathered together in the den. Dante called Wesley and repeated the information he had gotten again. After Wesley had finished, Dante told the group about having Angela having her people on Raul's trap house locations. Her people were on the north side and he himself would be casing the other spot. Continuing the discussion until sometime after 11:00 p.m., Dante ended the meeting. Just as they started clearing out, his phone rang.

Pulling out his phone, he read, 'Angela.' Dante headed toward the kitchen.

"Yeah Angela, what's up?" he answered.

"Hey baby, I'm leaving the station now are you coming to the house?"

"Yeah but not right now, it will be later on."

"Have you ate yet?"

"Nah," Dante answered looking over his shoulder only to see Alinna standing there watching him with a look that could kill.

"I'll pick us up something to eat. I love you papi."

"I know, but umm, let me call you back," Dante told Angela just as Alinna walked up to him.

"Who was that, Dante?" Alinna asked with an attitude as she stared up at him.

"It was Angela."

"We need to talk now," Alinna said after she rolled her eyes when hearing the other woman's name.

He followed Alinna upstairs, "Dante I have been thinking ..." Alinna started as she changed her clothes into one of his tee shirts.

"What about?" Dante asked as he changed clothes as well. Crawling into bed as Dante got in the other side, Alinna rolled over next to him exhaling a deep breath as he wrapped his arms around her.

"We have both been stressed out and dealing with all kinds of different things. How do you feel about going out of town, maybe even the country? You, me, and D.J."

Running his hands through her hair, Dante replied, "Yeah, I like that idea."

Smiling as she sat up and looked to him, "So we can go then?" Alinna asked excitedly. Pulling Alinna on top of him, as she straddled him, he took off the tee shirt.

Tossing it to the side as she smiled uncontrollably, "As soon as I deal with this Raul nigga, we out shorty," Dante told her. Alinna folded down and laid her body over his she turned her head and kissed him.

Mid-kiss she spoke with her lips still on his, "I love you so much Dante."

"And I love only you, Alinna. I swear on it," Dante told her rolling her on her back and positioning himself in between her legs.

$ $ $

Unable to sleep after making love to Dante, Alinna laid next on his chest unsure of how long she had been awake when she heard Dante tell Angela that he was on his way. Continuing to pretend to be asleep even after Dante hung up the phone with Angela and slid out of bed, Alinna laid listening to him move around the bedroom only to hear his keys a few moments later.

Waiting a moment before she opened her eyes and saw that Dante was gone, Alinna hopped out of bed and rushed to put on a pair of jeans. She took off Dante's t-shirt and slipped into her own along with some baby blue and white Air Max's. Snatching up her keys, gun, and purse, Alinna took off out of the bedroom, stopping at Rose's room to wake her up and let her know to listen out for D.J.

Making it downstairs just in time to see the headlights from Dante's Range Rover as he drove past the house, Alinna ran through the kitchen and into the garage, running to her BMW. Getting the garage door opened once she was in the car, Alinna cranked up the engine and backed out in a hurry.

Flying around the back of the house and then shooting past the front gate, Alinna punched the gas and picked up speed. Spotting the Range Rover ahead a few minutes later at a red light, Alinna slowed not wanting to get too close.

Trailing far enough behind the Range Rover to keep from sight, Alinna had been trailing Dante for nearly fifteen minutes when Dante finally pulled into a neighborhood. Alinna continued trailing him through the nice middle class neighborhood seeing him pull off to the side and park in front of a white and creamy brown house.

Parking the BMW two houses away and across the street from the house, Dante had rolled up to when Alinna saw the front door open. A Spanish woman stepped into the doorway wearing boy shorts and a men's wife beater.

Watching Dante climb out of the Range Rover, Alinna felt her heart picking up speed as she looked past her and around. Staring as Dante walked up to the porch, the Spanish woman wrapped her arms around his neck. Alinna gripped the steering wheel watching them greet one another and kiss.

"I'ma kill both of them."

TO BE CONTINUED...

BOOKS BY GOOD2GO AUTHORS

GOOD 2 GO FILMS PRESENTS

**THE HAND I WAS DEALT- FREE WEB SERIES
NOW AVAILABLE ON YOUTUBE!
YOUTUBE.COM/SILKWHITE212**

SEASON TWO NOW AVAILABLE

To order books, please fill out the order form below:

To order films please go to www.good2gofilms.com

Name:_____

Address:_____

City:_____ State:_____ Zip Code:_____

Phone:_____

Email:_____

Method of Payment: Check   VISA   MASTERCARD

Credit Card#:_____

Name as it appears on card:_____

Signature:_____

Item Name	Price	Qty	Amount
48 Hours to Die – Silk White	$14.99		
Business Is Business – Silk White	$14.99		
Business Is Business 2 – Silk White	$14.99		
Business Is Business 3 – Silk White	$14.99		
Childhood Sweethearts – Jacob Spears	$14.99		
Childhood Sweethearts 2 – Jacob Spears	$14.99		
Childhood Sweethearts 3 - Jacob Spears	$14.99		
Flipping Numbers – Ernest Morris	$14.99		
Flipping Numbers 2 – Ernest Morris	$14.99		
He Loves Me, He Loves You Not - Mychea	$14.99		
He Loves Me, He Loves You Not 2 - Mychea	$14.99		
He Loves Me, He Loves You Not 3 - Mychea	$14.99		
He Loves Me, He Loves You Not 4 – Mychea	$14.99		
He Loves Me, He Loves You Not 5 – Mychea	$14.99		
Lost and Turned Out – Ernest Morris	$14.99		
Married To Da Streets – Silk White	$14.99		
M.E.R.C. - Make Every Rep Count Health and Fitness	$14.99		
My Besties – Asia Hill	$14.99		
My Besties 2 – Asia Hill	$14.99		
My Besties 3 – Asia Hill	$14.99		
My Besties 4 – Asia Hill	$14.99		
My Boyfriend's Wife - Mychea	$14.99		
My Boyfriend's Wife 2 – Mychea	$14.99		
Never Be The Same – Silk White	$14.99		
Stranded – Silk White	$14.99		
Slumped – Jason Brent	$14.99		
Tears of a Hustler - Silk White	$14.99		
Tears of a Hustler 2 - Silk White	$14.99		
Tears of a Hustler 3 - Silk White	$14.99		
Tears of a Hustler 4- Silk White	$14.99		
Tears of a Hustler 5 – Silk White	$14.99		
Tears of a Hustler 6 – Silk White	$14.99		
The Panty Ripper - Reality Way	$14.99		
The Panty Ripper 3 – Reality Way	$14.99		

The Teflon Queen – Silk White	$14.99		
The Teflon Queen 2 – Silk White	$14.99		
The Teflon Queen 3 – Silk White	$14.99		
The Teflon Queen 4 – Silk White	$14.99		
The Teflon Queen 5 – Silk White	$14.99		
The Teflon Queen 6 - Silk White	$14.99		
Tied To A Boss - J.L. Rose	$14.99		
Time Is Money - Silk White	$14.99		
Young Goonz – Reality Way	$14.99		
Subtotal:			
Tax:			
Shipping (Free) U.S. Media Mail:			
Total:			

Make Checks Payable To:
Good2Go Publishing
7311 W Glass Lane,
Laveen, AZ 85339

CPSIA information can be obtained
at www.ICGtesting.com
Printed in the USA
LVOW04s1313290716
498316LV00024B/316/P